D1281194

The other birds laughed at him
because he was so tiny.

MOTHER WEST WIND "WHEN" STORIES

BY

THORNTON W. BURGESS

Illustrations by
HARRISON CADY

Amereon House
Mattituck

TO THE READER

It is our pleasure to keep available uncommon titles and to this end, at the time of publication, we have used the best available sources. To aid catalogers and collectors, this title is printed in an edition limited to 300 copies. ———**Enjoy!**

International Standard Book Number 0-8488-0387-6

To order contact:
AMEREON HOUSE,
the publishing division of AMEREON LTD.
Post Office Box 1200
Mattituck, NY 11952

Manufactured in the United States
by The Mad Printers of Mattituck

DEDICATION

To all little children and to all those crowned with the glory of many years who still retain that priceless possession, the heart of a child, this little volume is affectionately dedicated.

CONTENTS

LIST OF ILLUSTRATIONS

I

WHEN MR. BLUEBIRD WON HIS BEAUTIFUL COAT

OF all the joyous sounds of all the year there is none more loved by Peter Rabbit, and the rest of us for that matter, than the soft whistle of Winsome Bluebird in the spring. The first time Peter hears it he always jumps up in the air, kicks his long heels together, and does a funny little dance of pure joy, for he knows that Winsome Bluebird is the herald of sweet Mistress Spring, and that she is not far behind him. It is the end of the shivery, sad time and the beginning of the happy, glad time, and Peter rejoices when he hears that sweet, soft voice which is sometimes so hard to locate, seeming to come from everywhere and nowhere.

So Peter loves Winsome Bluebird and never tires of seeing him about. You know he wears a very, very beautiful coat of blue, the blue of the sky when it is softest, and you love to lie on your back and look up into it and dream and dream. It always has seemed to Peter that Winsome's coat is one of the loveliest he ever has seen, as indeed it is, and that it is quite right and proper and just as it should be that one having such a beautiful voice and bringing such a beautiful message should himself be beautiful. He said as much one day when he had run over to the Smiling Pool to pay his respects to Grandfather Frog.

"Chug-a-rum! Certainly. Of course," replied Grandfather Frog. "Winsome Bluebird has a beautiful nature and his beautiful coat is the reward which Old Mother Nature has given him. It has been in the family ever since his grandfather a thousand times removed was brave enough to become the herald of Mistress Spring."

"Oh, Grandfather Frog, that sounds like a story," cried Peter. "Please, please tell it to me, for I love Winsome Bluebird, and I know I shall love him more when I have learned more about him. His great-great-ever-so-great-grandfather must have done something very fine to have won such a lovely reward."

"He did," replied Grandfather Frog.

He became the herald of Mistress

Spring when no one else would, and bravely carried his message of gladness and joy where it was sadly needed, in spite of cold and hardship which no one else was willing to face."

"Please, please tell me all about it," begged Peter.

Grandfather Frog appeared to consider for a few minutes, and Peter waited anxiously. Then Grandfather Frog cleared his voice. "I will," said he, "because you ought to know it. Everybody ought to know it, and Winsome Bluebird certainly never will tell it himself. He is too modest for that. It happened a great while ago when the world was young. Mr. Bluebird was one of the quietest and most modest of all the birds. He wore just a modest gray coat, and no one took any particular notice of him. In fact, he didn't even have a name. He never quarreled with his neighbors. He never was envious of those to whom Old Mother Nature had given beautiful coats, or if he were, he never showed it. He just minded his own affairs and did his best to do his share of the work of the Great World, for even in the beginning of things there was something for each one to do.

"Old Mother Nature was very busy those days making the Great World a fit place in which to live, and as soon as she had started a new family of birds or animals she had to leave them to take care of themselves and get along as best they could. Those who were too lazy or too stupid to take care of themselves disappeared, and others took their places. There was nothing lazy or stupid about Mr. Bluebird, and he quickly learned how to take care of himself and at the same time to keep on the best of terms with his neighbors.

"When the place where the first birds lived became too crowded and old King Eagle led them out into the new land Old Mother Nature had been preparing for them, Mr. Bluebird was one of the first to follow him. The new land was very beautiful, and there was plenty of room and plenty to eat for all. Then came Jack Frost with snow and ice and drove all the birds back to the place they had come from. They made up their minds that they would stay there even if it were crowded. But after a while Old Mother Nature came to tell them that soon Jack Frost would be driven back from that wonderful new land, and sweet Mistress Spring would waken all the sleeping plants and all the sleeping insects up there so that it would be as beautiful as it was before, even more beautiful than the place where they were now. She said that she should expect them to go to the new land and make it joyous with their songs and build their homes there and help her to keep the insects and worms from eating all the green things.

" 'But first I want a herald to go before Mistress Spring to tell those who have lived there all through the time of snow and ice that Mistress Spring is coming. Who will go as the herald of sweet Mistress Spring?' asked Old Mother Nature.

" All the birds looked at one another and shivered, and then one by one they tried to slip out of sight. Now Mr. Bluebird had modestly waited for some of his big, strong neighbors to offer to take the message of gladness up into that frozen land, but when he saw them slip away one by one, his heart grew hot with shame for them, and he flew out before Old Mother Nature. 'I'll go,' said he, bobbing his head respectfully.

"Old Mother Nature just had to smile, because compared with some of his neighbors Mr. Bluebird was so very small. 'What can such a little fellow as you do?' she asked. 'You will freeze to death up there, for it is still very cold.'

"'If you please, I can at least try,' replied Mr. Bluebird modestly. 'If I find I can't go on, I can come back.'

"'And what reward do you expect?' asked Old Mother Nature.

"'The joy of spreading such good news as the coming of Mistress Spring will be is all the reward I want,' replied Mr. Bluebird.

"This reply so pleased Old Mother

Nature that she then and there made Mr. Bluebird the herald of Mistress Spring and started him on his long journey. It *was* a long journey and a hard journey, harder, very much harder for Mr. Bluebird than the same journey is for Winsome these days. You see, everything was new to him. And then it was so cold! He couldn't get used to the cold. It seemed sometimes as if he certainly would freeze to death. At these times, when he sat shivering and shaking, he would remember that sweet Mistress Spring was not very far behind and that he was her herald. This would give him courage, and he would bravely keep on. Whenever he stopped to rest, he would whistle the news that Mistress Spring was coming, and sometimes, just to keep up his own courage, he would whistle while he was flying. and he found it helped. To keep warm at night he crept into hollow trees, and it was thus he learned how snug and safe and comfortable such places were, and he made up his mind that in just such a place he would build his nest when the time came.

"As he passed on he left behind him great joy, and Mistress Spring found as she journeyed north that all in the forests and on the meadows were eagerly awaiting her, for they had heard the message of her coming; and she was glad and told Old Mother Nature how well her herald had done his work. When he had completed his errand, Mr. Bluebird built a home and was as modest and retiring as ever. He didn't seem to think that he had done anything out of the usual. He simply rejoiced in his heart that he had been able to do what Old Mother Nature had requested, and it never entered his head that he should have any other reward than the knowledge that he had done his best and that he had brought cheer and hope to many.

"When Jack Frost moved down from the far North in the fall, all the birds journeyed south again, and of course Mr. Bluebird went with them. The next season when it was time for Mistress Spring to start north, Old Mother Nature assembled all the birds, and this time, instead of asking who would carry the message, she called Mr. Bluebird out before them and asked if he were willing to be the herald once more. Mr. Bluebird said that he would be glad to be the herald if she wished it. Then Old Mother Nature told all the birds how brave Mr. Bluebird was and how faithful and true, and she made all the other birds feel ashamed, especially those bigger and stronger than Mr.

Bluebird. Then she said: 'Winsome Bluebird, for that is to be your name from now on, I here and now appoint you the herald of Mistress Spring, and the honor shall descend to your children and your children's children forever and ever, and you shall be one of the most loved of all the birds. And because you are a herald, you shall have a bright coat, as all heralds should have; and because you are true and faithful, your coat shall be blue, as blue as the blue of the sky.'

"She reached out and touched Mr. Bluebird, and sure enough his sober gray coat turned the most wonderful blue. Then once more he started on his long journey and he whistled his message more joyously than before. And because his whistle brought joy and gladness, and because he was beautiful to see, it came about just as Old Mother

Nature had said it would, that he was one of the most loved of all the birds, even as his great-great-ever-so-great-grandson is to-day."

Peter drew a long breath. "Thank you, Grandfather Frog," said he. "I have always loved Winsome Bluebird and now I shall love him more."

II

WHEN OLD MR. GOPHER FIRST GOT POCKETS

II

WHEN OLD MR. GOPHER FIRST GOT POCKETS

THERE was one of Peter Rabbit's neighbors of whose presence he was always aware, and yet whom he almost never saw. No, it wasn't Miner the Mole, but it was one who lives in much the same way as Miner. When Peter would leave the dear Old Briar-patch he seldom went far without coming to a little pile of fresh earth. These little piles of earth had puzzled Peter a great deal for a long time. It sometimes seemed to Peter as if they appeared by magic. He would pass across a certain part of the Green Meadows, and there would be nothing but the green things growing there. When he returned the same way, there would be one or two or maybe half a dozen piles of newly turned earth.

"Of course," said Peter the first time he noticed one of these little earth piles, "where there is a pile of earth like that, there must be a hole. Some one has been digging, and this is the dirt thrown out."

But when Peter looked for the hole he couldn't find one. There was no hole. It was very puzzling, but it was a fact. He kicked that pile of earth until he had scattered it far and wide, but there was no sign of a hole. Later he tried the same thing with other little piles of earth, but never once did he find a hole. It looked as if some one brought those little piles, dropped them on the Green Meadows, and then went away. Of course no one did anything of the kind, and Peter knew it. He spent a good deal of time wondering who could make them. Then one day, as he was hopping along across the Green Meadows, the ground right in front of him began to move. It so startled Peter that his first thought was to run. Then he decided that it would be foolish to run until there was something to run from. So he sat perfectly still and watched that spot where the ground was moving. Earth, loose earth, was pushed up from underneath, and even as Peter sat there staring, with eyes popping out of his head and mouth wide open in wonder, the pile grew and grew until it was as big as any of the piles about which he so often had wondered. Then suddenly a head was thrust out of the middle of it, a homely head. In an instant it vanished, and a second later the hole where it had been was filled. Peter could hear the stranger packing the earth in from underneath. When Peter had recovered his breath and looked, there was no sign of the hole. No one would ever have guessed that there had been one there.

That was Peter Rabbit's first meeting with Grubby Gopher. Since then he has seen Grubby several times, but Grubby is never what you would call neighborly, and Peter never has felt and never will feel really acquainted with him. But for one thing Peter would have thought Grubby Gopher the most uninteresting fellow he ever had met. The one thing was the discovery that Grubby has the biggest pockets in his cheeks that Peter has ever seen. And another thing about those pockets — they are on the *outside* of Grubby's cheeks instead of being inside, as is the case with Striped Chipmunk. When Peter discovered this, he became curious at once. Of course. Who wouldn't be curious? Peter felt sure that there must be a story in connection with those pockets. He wondered what use Grubby Gopher had for pockets, anyway. He wondered why they were outside instead of inside his cheeks. He wondered a great many things, did Peter. And when he just couldn't stand it any longer for wondering, he began to ask questions.

"Why does Grubby Gopher have pockets in his cheeks?" he asked Jimmy Skunk.

"Because they are handier there than they would be anywhere else," replied Jimmy with a twinkle in his eyes. "Have you seen any fat beetles this morning, Peter?"

"No," returned Peter shortly. Then

an idea came to him. "I tell you what, Jimmy," said he, speaking eagerly, "if you'll tell me about those queer pockets of Grubby's and how he came by them, I'll help you hunt for some beetles. Is it a bargain?"

Jimmy Skunk scratched his nose thoughtfully as if trying to decide which would have the better of the bargain. Then he grinned good-naturedly. You know, Jimmy really is one of the best-natured little people in the world. "All right," said he, "it's a bargain. You do your part and I'll do mine. Now where shall I begin?"

"Begin with the days when the world was young, of course," replied Peter. "All good stories seem to have had their beginnings then, so far as I can see. Of course Grubby got those pockets from his father, and his father got them from his father, and so on way back to the first Gopher. So begin right off with him."

"Just as you say," replied Jimmy. "Old Mr. Gopher, the first Gopher, who wasn't old then, was one of the little people whom Old Mother Nature turned loose in the Great World which was just in its beginning and told to make the best of life as they found it. No doubt they would need things which they hadn't got, but first they must find out what they really did need. Later, when she had more time, she would consider these needs, and if they were real needs, not just desires, she would see what could be done to supply them.

"So Mr. Gopher started out to make his way in the Great World, and it wasn't long before he discovered that everybody else was doing the same thing. It soon became clear to him that if everybody lived on the same kind of food, there wouldn't be enough to go around, and the biggest and strongest creatures would get all there was, leaving the smaller and weaker ones to starve. Not long after this he discovered certain of his big neighbors had begun to look at him in a way that made him most uncomfortable. In fact, they looked at him with such a hungry gleam in their eyes, and they licked their lips in such an unpleasant way whenever he met them, that little cold shivers ran all over him and he decided that the less he was seen the better his chances.

"One other thing Mr. Gopher discovered, and this was that each one seemed to have some special gift. One was a good climber, another a swift runner, a third a wonderful jumper, a fourth a great swimmer. Mr. Gopher could neither climb, nor run, nor jump, nor swim particularly well. What could he do? Somehow he had a feeling that Old Mother Nature had given him some special advantage. What could it be? He sat down and studied himself. Then he noticed for the first time that his hands were different from the hands of those about him. For his size they were very large and strong, and on the three middle fingers of each hand were long, stout claws. What could he do with these besides fight? Dig! That was it; he could dig. He tried it. Sure enough, he could dig at a surprising rate.

"Then came a new idea. He would dig himself a hole and live in it. That would keep him out of sight of his big neighbors with the hungry-looking eyes and the watery mouths. So he dug himself a hole, and then he discovered that in order to get food he must leave the hole, and so he was no better off than before. While he was studying over this, he started a little tunnel just for the fun of digging, for he liked to dig, did Mr. Gopher. Presently he came to a root in his path. He decided to cut it and get it out of his way. Now when he began to cut it he made another discovery, one that tickled him half to death. That root was good to eat! He ate all of it, and then he went on digging, hoping to find another. He did find another. Then Mr. Gopher made up his mind that in the future he would live underground and be safe. He would make himself a comfortable house, and then from that he would tunnel wherever he pleased for food.

"So Mr. Gopher made a comfortable house underground, and then he started digging for food. Every once in a while he would make an opening at the surface of the ground and push out the dirt he had dug in making his tunnel, filling up the opening as soon as he had pushed out all the dirt. In this way he kept his tunnels clear, so that he could run back and forth through them. So he lived very comfortably until one day he happened to overhear Mr. Squirrel talking about the coming of Jack Frost and telling how he wouldn't mind because he was laying up stores of food in a storehouse.

" 'That's a good idea of Mr. Squirrel's,' thought Mr. Gopher, who was much troubled by what he had heard about the coming of Jack Frost. 'I believe I'll do the same thing.' But when he tried it, he found it slow, hard work. You see, he could carry so little at a time, and had to carry it so far, that it was very discouraging. He had forgotten all about Old Mother Nature until suddenly one day she appeared before him and smilingly asked what boon she could grant him. Almost without thinking he replied, 'Pockets! Big pockets in my cheeks!'

"Old Mother Nature looked surprised. 'Tell me all about it,' said she. 'Why do you want pockets, and what would you do with them if you had them?'

"So Mr. Gopher explained to Old Mother Nature how he had learned to live underground and how lately he had been trying to lay up a store of food but had found it slow work.

"Old Mother Nature was pleased to think that Mr. Gopher had made the most of his opportunities, but she didn't say so. 'I'll think it over,' said she and left him. But the very next time Mr. Gopher brushed a hand against one of his cheeks, he discovered a great pocket there. Hastily he felt of the other.

There was another great pocket there! Then Mr. Gopher was perfectly happy. He felt that there wasn't a single thing in all the world that he could ask for to make him any happier. It is just the same way with Grubby to-day. He is perfectly happy working in the dark under the ground and very, very proud of the big pockets in his cheeks," concluded Jimmy Skunk.

"Thank you, Jimmy. Thank you ever so much. Now I'll help you find some fat beetles," cried Peter.

III

WHEN OLD MR. GROUSE GOT HIS SNOWSHOES

III

WHEN OLD MR. GROUSE GOT HIS SNOWSHOES

PETER RABBIT and Mrs. Grouse are very good friends. In fact they are the best of friends. For one thing they are very near neighbors. Once in a great while Mrs. Grouse comes to the dear Old Briar-patch and walks along Peter's private little paths. However, that isn't often. But up in the bramble tangle on the edge of the Green Forest they spend a great deal of time together. You see, they both fear the same enemies, and so they have a great deal to talk over, and each is always ready to help the other.

When winter comes Peter is sometimes rather lonely. You see, a lot of his feathered friends fly away to the warm, sunny Southland to spend the winter. Other friends, Johnny Chuck and Striped Chipmunk and Grandfather Frog for instance, retire and sleep all through the cold weather. Peter cannot understand what they do it for, but they do. So Peter has very few to gossip with after Jack Frost arrives. But he can always count on Mrs. Grouse. No matter how hard Jack Frost pinches, or how bitter the breath of rough Brother North Wind, somewhere in the Green Forest Mrs. Grouse is bravely doing her best to get enough to eat, and Peter knows that if he looks for her he will find her.

There was one thing about Mrs. Grouse that puzzled Peter for a long time, and this was the difference between the footprints she made in the soft damp earth after a rain in the summer and the prints she made in the snow. The first time he noticed those prints in the snow, he actually didn't know who had made them. You know how very, very curious Peter is. He followed those queer footprints, and when he found that they led right straight into the bramble tangle, he just didn't know what to think. He sat down on the edge of the bramble tangle and scratched his long right ear with his long left hind foot. When Peter does this it is a sign that he is very much puzzled about something.

"Good morning, Peter Rabbit. You seem to have something on your mind," said a voice from the middle of the bramble tangle.

Peter gave a little start of surprise. Then he hopped into the bramble tangle along one of the little paths he had cut there. "Good morning, Mrs. Grouse," he replied. "I *have* got something on my mind. I have been following some strange tracks, and I don't know what to make of them." He pointed at one of them as he spoke.

"Oh," replied Mrs. Grouse in a tone of great surprise. "I made those with my snowshoes. I supposed you knew."

"Snowshoes! What are snow-shoes?" asked Peter, looking more puzzled than ever.

Very proudly Mrs. Grouse held out one foot for Peter to look at. Instead of the slim smooth toes he often had admired Peter saw that the bottom of each was covered for its whole length with queer-looking, horny little points that prevented the foot from sinking way down in the snow as it would have done without them. This made it very easy for Mrs. Grouse to get about on the snow instead of having to wade through it.

"My!" exclaimed Peter. "How perfectly splendid! Where did you get them?"

"Oh," replied Mrs. Grouse with pride in her voice, "they have been in the family a great many years. They were given to my great-great-ever-so-great-grandfather by Old Mother Nature."

"Tell me about it. Do please tell me about it," begged Peter, who had not had a story since Grandfather Frog went to sleep for the winter.

Mrs. Grouse fluffed out her feathers and settled herself comfortably. "There isn't much to tell," she began, "but all the same our family always has been rather proud of the way we came by our snowshoes. It all happened a great while ago."

"Way back in the time that Grandfather Frog tells about, when the world was young?" interrupted Peter.

Mrs. Grouse nodded and went on. "Great-grandfather Grouse lived very comfortably in those days, even when the hard times came and so many took to killing their neighbors because food was scarce. He always managed to get enough to eat because he didn't believe in being fussy. When he couldn't get what he wanted, he took what he could get and was thankful. When he couldn't find grasshoppers or crickets or bugs of any kind, or chestnuts or beechnuts or berries that he liked, he ate such berries as he could find, whether he liked them or not; and when he couldn't find berries or seeds, he ate the buds of trees. So one way or another he managed to pick up a living and to keep out of the way of his enemies, for he was just as smart as they were. You know, in those days there were no hunters with dreadful guns.

"So Grandfather Grouse managed to get along without really suffering until the coming of the first snow. That first snow was hard on everybody, but it was particularly hard on Grandfather Grouse. His slim toes cut right through. They wouldn't hold him up at all. Of course he spent as much time as possible up in the trees, but when he wanted to get low-hanging berries on the bushes, the kind that stay on all winter, you know, he just had to stand on the ground and reach up for them. Then, too, his feet were intended for walking and running rather than for perching in trees, and it made his toes ache dreadfully to have to cling to the branch of a tree too long. I know just how it felt because I have had to do it when Reddy Fox has been hunting for me.

" But Grandfather Grouse made the best of a bad matter and didn't say a word, not a word. He waded around in the snow as best he could, but it was dreadfully tiresome. He couldn't take more than a few steps without stopping to rest. And this wasn't all; the snow made his feet ache with the cold. He had to keep drawing first one foot and then the other up to warm them in his feathers.

" Now Grandfather Grouse had sharp eyes, and he knew how to use them. He had to, to keep out of danger. He watched the other little people, and he soon saw that those with big feet, feet that were big for the size of their bodies, didn't sink in like those with small, slim feet. For the first time in his life he began to wish that Old Mother Nature had made him different. He wished that he had broad feet. Yes, Sir, he wished just that. Then a thought popped into his head. Perhaps the snow wasn't going to last forever. Perhaps it would go away and never come again. Then he wouldn't want broad feet, but just the kind of feet he already had. He sighed. Then he tried to smile bravely.

" 'I guess,' said he, talking out loud to himself, for he thought he was quite alone, 'I guess the thing to do is to stop worrying about the things I haven't got and make the most of the blessings I have got,' and he started to wade through the snow for some berries just ahead.

" Now Old Mother Nature happened to be passing, and she overheard Grandfather Grouse. 'I wish that every one felt as you do,' said she. 'It would make things a great deal easier for me. But what is it that you wish you had?'

"Grandfather Grouse felt both pleased and a little ashamed — ashamed that he should even *seem* to be dissatisfied. At first he tried to pretend that everything really was all right, but after a little urging he told Old Mother Nature all about his troubles since the coming of the snow. She listened and looked thoughtful. Then she told Grandfather Grouse to be patient and perhaps things would not be so bad as they seemed. Somehow Grandfather Grouse felt better after that, and when he went to bed for the night in a big hemlock-tree he was almost cheerful.

"The next morning when he flew down to get his breakfast, he had the greatest surprise of his life. Instead of sinking way down into the snow, he sank hardly at all. He could get about with the greatest ease. He didn't know what to make of it until he happened to look down at his feet and then he saw —"

"That he had snowshoes!" interrupted Peter Rabbit, dancing about in great excitement.

"Just so," replied Mrs. Grouse. "He had snowshoes just like the ones I have now. When spring came, Old Mother Nature came around and took them away, because he no longer had need of them; but when the next winter came, she returned them to him. She called them the reward of patience. And ever since that long-ago day our family has had snowshoes in the winter. I really don't know how we would get along without them."

"I don't know how you would," replied Peter Rabbit. "Isn't it splendid how Old Mother Nature seems to know just what everybody needs?"

And with that Peter started for the dear Old Briar-patch to tell little Mrs. Peter all about the snowshoes of Mrs. Grouse.

IV

WHEN OLD MR. PANTHER LOST HIS HONOR

IV

WHEN OLD MR. PANTHER LOST HIS HONOR

PETER RABBIT, always curious, had overheard his cousin, Jumper the Hare, tell Prickly Porky the Porcupine that it was lucky for him Puma the Panther was too much afraid of men to come down to the Green Forest to live, but kept to the Great Woods and the Big Mountains. At the very mention of Puma the thousand little spears of Prickly Porky had rattled together, and Peter had a queer feeling that this time, instead of being rattled purposely to make others afraid, they rattled because Prickly Porky himself shook with something very like fear. In fact, it seemed to Peter that Prickly Porky actually turned pale.

Now Peter knew nothing at all about Puma the Panther, and right away he was so full of questions that he could hardly wait to get Jumper alone so that he might satisfy his curiosity. The first chance he got he began to ask questions so fast that Jumper clapped his hands over both ears and threatened to run away.

"Who is Puma? Where does he live? Why is Prickly Porky afraid of him? What does he look like? Why —" It was then that Jumper clapped his hands over his ears. Peter grinned. "Please, Cousin Jumper, tell me about him," he begged.

Jumper pretended to consider for a few minutes. Then, because like most people he likes to air his knowledge, and also because he is very fond of his cousin Peter, he told him what he knew about Puma the Panther.

"In the first place," said he, "Puma is the biggest member of the Cat family living in the Great Woods."

"Is he bigger than Tufty the Lynx?" asked Peter eagerly.

Jumper nodded, and Peter's eyes opened very wide. "He looks very much like Black Pussy, Farmer Brown's cat, only he is yellowish-brown instead of black, and is ever and ever and ever so many times bigger," continued Jumper. "He has a long tail, just like Black Pussy, and great claws which are terribly sharp. He is so soft-footed that he can steal through the woods without making a sound; he can climb trees like Happy Jack Squirrel, and he is so big and strong that every one but Buster Bear is afraid of him, even

Prickly Porky, for he is so smart and cunning that he has found a way to make Prickly Porky's thousand little spears quite useless to protect him. But big and strong and smart as he is, he is a coward because he is a sneak, and all sneaks are cowards. Of course, you know that, Peter."

Peter nodded. "Everybody knows that," said he. "But if he is so big and strong and smart, why is he a sneak?"

"I guess it's in his blood, and he can't help himself," replied Jumper. "I guess it is because way back in the beginning of things his great-great-ever-so-great-grandfather lost his honor, and none of the family ever has got it back again."

"How did old Mr. Panther lose his honor?" demanded Peter, fairly itching with curiosity and eagerness.

"Well," replied Jumper, "all I know is what I've heard whispered about among the people of the Great Woods. It may be true and it may not be, but every one seems to believe it. As I said before, it happened way back in the beginning of things. Old King Bear ruled the Great Woods then, and there was peace between all the animals. Mr. Panther was sleek and handsome and graceful in all his movements. He knew it, too. He spent a great deal of time washing himself and smoothing his fur, just as Black Pussy does. He would stretch out in the sun for hours with his eyes closed until they were just slits. But all the time he saw all that was going on around him.

"He would watch old King Bear shuffling about in his clumsy fashion, and he would curl the end of his tail up and twitch it scornfully. Then he would look at his own trim form admiringly and think how much finer-looking a king he would make. The more he watched old King Bear, the more this feeling grew. He became envious and then jealous. But he took care never to let old King Bear know this. You see, there was one thing about King Bear which Mr. Panther did respect, and that was his strength. He had no desire to quarrel with King Bear. So whenever they met he was very polite and said flattering things to him. But behind his back Mr. Panther made fun of him, but did it in such an artful way that his neighbors merely thought that they themselves were making the discovery of how much handsomer Mr. Panther was than old King Bear.

"After a while came the hard time when food was scarce, and in order to keep from starving, the big and strong began to prey on their neighbors who were smaller or weaker or more helpless. But the law was made that none should kill more than was needed to fill an empty stomach for the time being. It was then that Mr. Panther thought of a plan for making old King Bear hated by all his subjects.

"'If they hate him, they will refuse to have him as king any longer, and I, being next in strength and far more kingly in appearance, will be made king in his place,' reasoned Mr. Panther, but he took care not to hint such a thing.

"Presently ugly stories began to float about. Some one was killing seemingly for the fun of killing. It was dreadful, but it was true. Almost every day some one was found killed but not eaten, and always there were footprints going to and away from the place, and they were the footprints of *old King Bear!* So all the forest people began to hate King Bear and to mutter among themselves that they would have him for king no longer. Finally some of them went to Old Mother Nature and told her all about it; they asked that old King Bear be punished and that some one else be made king in his place. Old Mother Nature told them that she would think it over.

"Quite unknown to old King Bear, she followed him about and watched him as he shuffled about in his clumsy way. 'Hm-m, it ought not to be very hard to keep out of his way. Those who are caught must be very stupid if *he* catches them,' thought she. Presently her sharp eyes caught a glimpse of a shadowy form sneaking along behind old King Bear. It was Mr. Panther, and he was stepping with the greatest care so as to leave no footprints. Old

Mother Nature sat down and waited. She saw Mr. Panther bound away through the trees. By and by he came back, bringing the body of a Hare which he had killed. He laid it down where old King Bear had left a footprint in the soft earth and then, with his long tail twitching, he looked this way and that way to make sure that no one had seen him and then bounded away.

"The next day Old Mother Nature called all the people of the forest before her, and they all came, for none dared stay away. When they were all there, she had each in turn look her straight in the face while she asked if they had hunted fairly and honorably and only when they were hungry. Each in turn looked her straight in the face and said that he had until it came the turn of Mr. Panther. Mr. Panther's tail twitched nervously, and he looked everywhere but at Old Mother Nature as she put the question to him.

"'Look me straight in the face and tell me on your honor that you have hunted fairly,' commanded Old Mother Nature. Mr. Panther knew that all eyes were upon him, and he tried his best to look her in the face, but he couldn't do it. You see, he hadn't any honor. He had lost it, and without honor no one can look another straight in the face. Instead he turned and began to slink away, and all who saw him wondered how they ever could have thought him kingly-looking.

"Then Old Mother Nature told what she had seen the day before, and at once everybody understood who it was that had been doing the killing and trying to make it appear that it was old King Bear, and they all turned and shouted 'Coward! Sneak! Coward! Sneak!'

until Mr. Panther fairly ran to get out of hearing. From that time on he lived by himself and would not look even timid Mr. Hare in the face. Instead of hunting openly and boldly like Mr. Wolf, he sneaked about in the forest and hunted by stealth, so that all the people of the forest looked on him with scorn, and though most of them feared him, they called him a coward and they nicknamed him 'Sneak-cat.'

"And to this day all Panthers have been the same, sneaking and cowardly in spite of their great size and strength, for it has been in their blood ever since the time when old Mr. Panther lost his honor," ended Jumper.

Peter was silent for a minute. Then he said softly: "I'm little and timid, but I'd rather be that way than to be big like Puma but a coward and a sneak. I can look any one in the face."

V

WHEN OLD MR. RAT BECAME AN OUTCAST

V

WHEN OLD MR. RAT BECAME AN OUTCAST

ROBBER THE BROWN RAT is an outcast among the little people of the Green Meadows and the Green Forest. You know an outcast is one with whom no one else will have anything to do. No one speaks to Robber. Whoever meets him pretends not to even see him, unless it happens to be one of the Hawk family or one of the Owl family or Shadow the Weasel. If one of these sees him, it is well for Robber to find a safe hiding-place without any loss of time.

But the rest of the little meadow and forest people turn their backs on Robber and get out of his way, partly because many of them are afraid of him, and partly because they despise him and consider him quite beneath them. He hasn't a single friend among them, not even among his own relatives. The latter are ashamed of him. If they could help it, they wouldn't even admit that they are related to him. Just mention him to them, and right away they will begin to talk about something else. Wag the Wood Rat and Bounder the Kangeroo Rat are very different fellows and are well liked, but Robber the Brown Rat is hated. Yes, Sir, he is hated even by his own relatives, which, you will agree, is a dreadful state of affairs.

Peter Rabbit had heard of Robber but never had seen him until one moonlight night he happened to go up to

Farmer Brown's barn just out of curiosity. He saw a hole under the barn and was trying to decide whether or not to go in and find out what was inside when who should come out but Robber himself. His coat was so rough and untidy, he was so dirty, he smelled so unclean, and he looked so savage that Peter at once decided that he wasn't interested in that barn and took himself off to the Green Forest, lipperty-lipperty-lip, as fast as he could go. All the rest of the night he thought about Robber the Brown Rat, and the very next day he hurried over to the Smiling Pool to ask Grandfather Frog how it was that Robber had become such a disreputable fellow with not a single friend.

Grandfather Frog had had a good breakfast of foolish green flies and was feeling in the very best of humor.

"Chug-a-rum!" said he, "Robber the Brown Rat is an outcast because he is all bad. His father was all bad, and his father's father, and so on way back to the beginning of things when the world was young. There was no good in any of them, and there is no good in Robber. He is a disgrace to the whole race of meadow and forest people, and so he lives only where man lives, and I have heard that he is as much hated by man as by the rest of us.

"Way back when the world was young, his great-great-ever-so-great-grandfather, who was the first of his race, lived with the rest of the little people in the Green Forest, and Old Mother Nature gave him the same chance to make an honest living that she gave to the rest. For a while Mr. Rat was honest. He was honest just as long as it was easier to be honest than dishonest. But when the hard times came of which you know, and food became scarce, Mr. Rat was too lazy to even try to earn his own living. He discovered that it was easier to steal from his neighbors. He wasn't at all particular whom he stole from, but he took from big and little alike. He was so sly about it that for a long time no one found him out.

"By and by his neighbors began to wonder how it was that Mr. Rat always seemed fat and well fed and yet never was seen to work. But Mr. Rat was too crafty to be caught stealing. He said he didn't need much to live on, which was an untruth, for he was a very greedy fellow. Now laziness is a habit that grows. First Mr. Rat was too lazy to work for his living. Then, little by little, he grew too lazy to be crafty. He grew bolder and bolder in his stealing, until at last he just took what he pleased from those who were smaller than he. Being well fed, he was strong. All the little people of his own size and smaller feared him. The bigger people said it was no business of theirs, so long as he didn't steal from them. All the time he *was* stealing from them, but hadn't been caught.

"Finally he grew too lazy to keep himself looking neat. His coat was always unbrushed and untidy-looking. He was always dirty. You see, it was too much work to even wash his face and hands. There was always food sticking to his whiskers. The little people kept away from him because they were afraid of him. The bigger people would have nothing to do with him because they were ashamed of him, ashamed to be seen in his company.

"So lazy Mr. Rat grew dirtier in his

The bigger people would have nothing to do with him, because they were ashamed of him.

habits, bolder in his stealing, and impudent to everybody. He became quarrelsome. It was about this time that the bigger people found him out.

"Mr. Lynx had secured the first meal he had had in a week. Part of it he put away for the next day. Before going to bed he went to have a look at it. Some of it was gone.

"'That's queer,' muttered Mr. Lynx. 'I wonder who there is who dares to steal from me.'

"Mr. Lynx hid where he could watch what was left of that meal. By and by he grew sleepy. He was just dozing off when he heard a noise. There was Mr. Rat carrying off part of what was left of that meal. With a snarl of anger Mr. Lynx leaped out. But Mr. Rat was too quick for him. He slipped into a hole. Mr. Lynx grabbed at him and caught him by the tail. Mr. Rat pulled and Mr. Lynx pulled. But Mr. Rat's tail was slippery, and Mr. Lynx couldn't hold on. He did, however, pull all the hair from it.

"Of course, Mr. Lynx told what had happened, and after that Mr. Rat did not dare show himself at all when the bigger people were about. So he lived in holes and continued to steal. Finally old King Bear called a meeting, and it was decided to drive Mr. Rat out of the Green Forest and off the Green Meadows. Little Mr. Weasel said that he was not afraid of Mr. Rat, and he would go into all the holes and drive Mr. Rat out. So Mr. Weasel went into hole after hole until at last he found Mr. Rat. Mr. Rat tried to fight, but he found that little Mr. Weasel was so slim and could move so quickly that he couldn't get hold of him. So at last Mr. Rat was forced to run to save his life.

"The minute he appeared all the others, big and little, started for him. Mr. Rat gave one look, and then, with a squeal of fright, he ran with all his might, dodging into one hiding-place after another, only to be chased out of each. And so at last he turned away from the Green Forest and the Green Meadows and ran to the homes of men, where he hid in dark places and stole from men as he formerly had stolen from his neighbors of the Green Forest. And because men are wasteful and allow much food to spoil, Mr. Rat found plenty to fill his stomach, such as it was, but often it was such as no one else would have touched.

"Once or twice he tried to get back to the Green Forest, but as soon as he was discovered he was driven back, and at last he gave up trying. He grew more dirty than ever, and finding everybody, even man, against him, he became savage of temper, living wholly by stealing, evil to look at and evil to come near, for in the dirt of his coat he carried sickness from place to place. In no place in all the Great World could he find a welcome.

"His children followed in his footsteps, and his children's children. Old Mother Nature became so disgusted with them that she said that they should always remain outcasts until they should mend their ways. But this they never did, and so Robber the Brown Rat is an outcast to-day, looked down on and hated by every living thing. There is none to say a good word for him. And to this day the tails of Robber's family have been almost bare of hair as a reminder of how old Mr. Rat of long ago came to be driven out of the Green Forest. Now are you satisfied, Peter Rabbit?" concluded Grandfather Frog.

"Yes, indeed, and I thank you ever so much," declared Peter. "Ugh! It must be dreadful to be despised and hated by all the Great World. I wouldn't be in Robber's place for anything."

"Chug-a-rum! I should hope not!" said Grandfather Frog.

VI

MR. MOOSE LOSES HIS HORNS

VI

WHEN MR. MOOSE LOST HIS HORNS

PETER RABBIT had just seen Flathorns the Moose for the first time, and Peter was having hard work to believe that there wasn't something the matter with his eyes. Indeed they looked as if something was the matter with them, for they seemed about to pop right out of his head. If any one had *told* Peter that any one as big as Flathorns lived in the Great Woods, he wouldn't have believed it, but now that he had *seen* that it was so, he just had to believe. So Peter sat with his eyes popping out and his mouth gaping wide open in the most foolish way as he stared in the direction in which Flathorns had gone.

"Big, isn't he?"

Peter looked up to see Blacky the Crow in the top of a birch-tree just at one side, and Blacky, too, was looking after Flathorns. Then Blacky looked down at Peter and began to laugh. "Don't try to swallow him, Peter!" said he.

Peter closed his mouth with a snap. "My, but he *is* big!" he exclaimed. "I never felt so small in all my life as when I first caught sight of him. What queer horns he has! I suppose they are horns, for he carries them on his head just as Lightfoot the Deer does his. They are so big I should think they would make his head ache."

"Perhaps they do, and that is why he drops them every spring and grows a new pair during the summer," replied Blacky.

"Drops them! Drops those great

horns and grows new ones in a single summer! Do you mean to tell me that hard things like those horns grow? And what do you mean by saying that he drops them every spring? Why, I saw him banging them against a tree just now, and I guess if they ever were coming off they would have come off then. You can't fool me with any such story as that, Blacky!"

"Have it your own way, Peter," replied Blacky. "Some people never can believe a thing until they see it with their own eyes. All I've got to say is just keep an eye on Flathorns in the spring and then remember what I've told you." Before Peter could reply Blacky had spread his wings, and with a harsh "Caw, caw, caw," had flown away.

Of course, after that Peter was very very curious about Flathorns the

Moose, and he just ached all over to ask about those horns. But every time he saw them the idea that they ever would or could come off seemed so impossible that he held his tongue. You see, he didn't want to be laughed at. So the winter passed, and Peter was no wiser than before. Then the spring came, and one never-to-be-forgotten day Peter was hurrying along, lipperty-lipperty-lip, when right in front of him lay something that made him stop short and stare even harder than he had stared the first time he saw Flathorns. What was it? Why, it was one of those very horns he had thought so much about! Yes, Sir, that is just what it was.

Even then Peter couldn't believe it was so. He couldn't believe it until he had hunted up Flathorns himself and seen with his own eyes that there were no longer any horns on that great head. Then Peter *had* to believe. It seemed to Peter the strangest thing he ever had heard of. There must be a reason, and if there were, Grandfather Frog would be sure to know it. So every day Peter visited the Smiling Pool to see if Grandfather Frog had wakened from his long winter sleep. At last one day he found him and could hardly wait to tell him how glad he was to see him once more and to be properly polite before he asked him about those horns of Flathorns the Moose.

"Chug-a-rum!" said Grandfather Frog. "It's pretty early in the season to be asking me for a story, but seeing it is you, Peter, and that you've waited all winter for it, I'll tell it to you. Way, way back in the days when the world was young, the first Moose, the great-great-ever-so-great-grandfather of Flathorns, was the biggest of all the animals in the Green Forest, but he had no horns, and he was such a homely fellow that everybody laughed at him and made fun of him. Now nothing hurts quite so much as being laughed at."

"I know," interrupted Peter.

"Mr. Moose felt so badly about it that he used to hide away and keep out of sight all he possibly could," continued Grandfather Frog. "Big as he was and strong as he was, he would turn and run away to hide from even such little people as Mr. Skunk and Mr. Squirrel and your ever-so-great-grandfather, Mr. Rabbit. He just couldn't bear to be laughed at. Old Mother Nature kept her eye on him and at last she took pity on him and crowned his head with the most wonderful horns, horns so big that no one smaller than

Mr. Moose could possibly have carried them.

"Then Mr. Moose threw up his head and carried it proudly, for now no one laughed at him. He marched through the Great Woods boldly, and even old King Bear, who was king no longer, stepped aside respectfully. Then pride entered into Mr. Moose; pride in his wonderful horns; pride in his great strength. He feared no one. He beat the bushes with his great horns and bellowed until the Great Woods rang with his voice, and all those who had once laughed at him hid in fear. He proclaimed himself king of the Great Woods, and no one dared to deny it.

"So he came and went when and where he pleased and felt himself every inch a king and carried his great horns as a crown. One day in the beginning of the springtime, he came face to face with Old Mother Nature. Once he would have bowed to her very humbly, but by now he had grown so proud and haughty that instead of stepping aside for her to pass, he boldly marched on with his head held high as if he did not see her. It was Old Mother Nature who stepped aside. She said nothing, but as he passed she reached forth and touched his great horns and they fell from his head, and with them fell all his pride and haughtiness. At once some of his neighbors who had been hiding near and had seen all that had happened began to mock him and make fun of him and laugh at him.

"Then, with his head hung low in shame, did Mr. Moose slink away and hide as he had done in the beginning, and none could find him save Old Mother Nature. Very humble was Mr. Moose when she visited him; all his pride was melted away in shame. Old Mother Nature was sorry for him. She promised him that he should have new horns, but that once a year he should lose his horns lest he should forget and again become over-proud and haughty. So while he kept hidden, the new horns grew and grew until they were greater and more wonderful than the ones he had had before. Then Mr. Moose once more came forth, holding his head high and glorying in his strength, and all his neighbors treated him with the greatest respect, quite as if he were really king of the Great Woods.

"But he never forgot what Old Mother Nature had said to him, and when the spring came, he slipped away and hid lest he should be seen without the glory of his horns, for in his heart he knew that Old Mother Nature would keep her word. Sure enough, his great horns dropped off, and in humbleness and patience he waited for new horns to grow. So it was all the years of his life, and so it has been with his children and his grandchildren even to this day, and so it is with Flathorns, and so it will be with his children. And the Moose family never have forgotten and never can forget that there is nothing so foolish as pride in personal appearance."

"Is that all?" asked Peter, as Grandfather Frog stopped.

"Isn't that enough?" demanded Grandfather Frog testily. "Just think it over a while, and when you are tempted to be proud and haughty just remember the horns of Mr. Moose and what happened to them."

"Thank you ever so much for the story," replied Peter politely as he hopped away. Half way to the dear Old

Briar-patch he paused. "It served old Mr. Moose just right!" he declared to no one in particular. And so it did.

VII

WHEN MR. KINGFISHER TOOK TO THE GROUND

VII

WHEN MR. KINGFISHER TOOK TO THE GROUND

PETER RABBIT had taken it into his funny little head to wander down the Laughing Brook below the Smiling Pool. It was open there, and in one place the bank was quite high and steep. Peter sat down on the edge of it and looked down. Right under him the Laughing Brook was very quiet and clear. Peter sat gazing down into it. He could see all the pebbles on the bottom and queer little plants growing among them. It seemed very queer, very queer indeed to Peter that plants, real plants, could be growing down there under water. Somehow he couldn't make it seem right that anything but fish should be able to live down there.

So Peter sat gazing down, lost in a sort of day-dream. The Jolly Little Sunbeams made beautiful lights and shadows in the water. Everything was so peaceful and beautiful that Peter quite forgot he was sitting right out in the open where Redtail the Hawk might spy him. He just gave himself up to dreams, day-dreams, you know. Presently those day-dreams were very, very near to being sleep-dreams. Yes, Sir, they were. Peter actually was nodding. His big eyes would close, open, close again, open and then close for a little longer. Suddenly a sharp and very loud noise, which seemed to come from right under his very toes, put an end to all nodding and dreaming. It was a long, harsh rattle, and it startled Peter so that he almost jumped out of his skin. Anyway, he jumped straight up in the air, and the wonder was that he didn't tumble headfirst down that steep bank right into the Laughing Brook. A queer prickly feeling ran all over him. He blinked his eyes rapidly. Then he saw a handsome blue and white and gray bird, with a head that looked too big for his body, flying up the Laughing Brook just above the water, and as he flew he made that sharp, harsh, rattling noise which had startled Peter so. Abruptly he paused in his flight, hovered over the water an instant, shot down, and disappeared with a tinkling little splash. A second later he was in the air again, and in his stout, spear-like bill was a gleaming, silvery thing. It was a little fish, a minnow.

"Rattles the Kingfisher!" exclaimed Peter, as he watched him fly over to a tree, pound the fish on a branch, and then go through the funniest performance as he tried to swallow the minnow whole. "Now where did he come from?" continued Peter. "It certainly seemed to me that he came from right under my very feet, but there isn't so much as a twig down there."

Peter poked his head over the edge of the bank. No, there wasn't a single thing down there on which Rattles could have been sitting. He was still wondering about it when his wobbly little nose caught a smell, a very unpleasant smell. It was the smell of fish, and it seemed to come from right under him. He leaned a little farther over the edge of the bank, and then he gave a funny little gasp. There was a *hole* in the bank only a few inches below him, and the smell certainly came from that hole.

Could it be, could it possibly be that Rattles had come out of that hole? It certainly seemed so, and yet Peter couldn't quite believe it. The very idea of a bird living in a hole in the ground!

"I don't believe it! I don't, so there!" exclaimed Peter right out loud.

"What is it you don't believe?" asked a voice. Peter looked down. There was Little Joe Otter looking up at him from the water, his eyes twinkling.

"I don't believe that Rattles the Kingfisher came out of that hole, yet I don't see where else he could have come from," replied Peter.

Little Joe chuckled. "That's where he came from, even if you don't believe it," said he. "I don't suppose you will believe that he dug that hole himself, either."

Peter's eyes opened very wide. "I—I'll believe it if you say on your honor that it really is so," he replied slowly.

"On my honor it really is so," said Little Joe Otter, his eyes twinkling more than ever. "Perhaps you would like to know how the great-great-grandfather of Rattles the Kingfisher happened to take the ground for a home."

Peter's eyes fairly danced. "Do tell me, Little Joe! Oh, please tell me!" he exclaimed.

Little Joe climbed out of the water on a rock just below Peter and settled himself comfortably.

"Once upon a time," he began.

"In the beginning of things," prompted Peter.

"Yes, in the beginning of things," replied Little Joe, "way back when the world was young, lived the very first of the Kingfisher family. From the very beginning Mr. Kingfisher was a very independent fellow. He cared nothing about his neighbors. That is, he was not social. He was polite enough, but he preferred his own company and was never happier than when he was by himself. Of course, his neighbors soon found this out. They called him odd and queer, and soon refused to even speak to him. This just suited Mr. Kingfisher, and he went about his business very well content to be let alone. He spent his days fishing, and, because there were few other fishermen, he always had plenty to eat. At night he found a comfortable roost in a tree, and so for a time he was perfectly contented.

"By and by he discovered that most of his neighbors were building homes.

At first he gave little attention to this, but after a while, seeing how happy they were, he began to think about a home for himself. The more he thought about it, the more he wanted one. But underneath Mr. Kingfisher's pointed cap were very clever wits. He would do nothing hastily. So he flew up and down the brook, appearing to do nothing but fish, but all the time he was keeping his eyes open, and there were no sharper eyes than those of Mr. Kingfisher.

"He was watching his neighbors work to see where and how they made their homes. He saw some of the birds building nests in the trees, some building them in the bushes, and a few building right on the ground.

"Of all he saw he liked best the home of Drummer the Woodpecker. 'That fellow has the right idea,' thought he.

'He cuts a hole in a tree; he is dry; he is warm; and no one can get at him there. If I build a home, that is the kind of place I want. He has got what I call plain sense, plain common sense!'

"After this Mr. Kingfisher watched until he was quite sure that no one was around to see him, and then he tried to make a hole in a tree as he had seen Drummer the Woodpecker do. But right away he discovered that two things were wrong; his bill was not made for cutting wood, and his feet were not big enough or the right shape for clinging to the side of a tree. Mr. Kingfisher was disappointed, very much disappointed. A hole seemed to him the only kind of a place for a home. He was thinking it over when he happened to discover Mr. Muskrat digging a hole in the bank. At first he didn't pay much attention. Then all in a flash an idea, a wonderful idea, came to him. Why shouldn't he have a home in the ground? No one in the wide world would ever think of looking for the home of a bird in the ground. With a rattle of joy, Mr. Kingfisher flew off up the brook to a steep, sandy bank of which he knew.

"'Just the place! Just the very place!' he cried. 'I'll make a hole just a little way from the top. No one will see it except from below, and it will be hard work for any one to climb up that sandy bank.'

"He flew straight at the spot he had selected and drove his big spear-like bill into it. Then he did it again and again. That bill wouldn't cut wood like the bill of Drummer the Woodpecker, but it certainly would cut into a sandy bank. In a little while he had room to cling with his feet. Then he could work faster and more easily. Pretty soon he had a hole deep enough to get into. He would looser the earth with his bill and scrape it out with his feet. He was so pleased with his discovery that he kept right on working. He almost forgot to eat. All the time he could spare from fishing, he spent digging. Day after day he worked. When he had a hole three or four feet straight into the bank, he made a turn in it and then kept on digging. When he had gone far enough in, he made a little bedroom.

"At last the house was done. Mr. Kingfisher chuckled happily. No one could get at him there. He had the best and safest home he knew of. It was better than the home of Drummer the Woodpecker. If Mr. Mink happened to find it, and Mr. Kingfisher could think of no one else who would be likely to, there would be nothing to fear, for Mr. Mink would never dare face that sharp bill in such a narrow place.

"It all worked out just as Mr. Kingfisher thought it would. No one dreamed of looking in the ground for his home, and for a long, long time he kept his secret so well that his neighbors thought he had no home, and called him 'Rattles the Homeless.' From that day to this the Kingfishers have made their homes in the ground," concluded Little Joe Otter.

"Isn't it wonderful?" exclaimed Peter, as he watched Rattles dive into the water and catch a silvery minnow. "I didn't know that any one wearing feathers had so much sense."

"There's a great deal you don't know, Peter," replied Little Joe Otter, sliding into the water.

VIII

WHEN OLD MR. BADGER LEARNED TO STAY AT HOME

VIII

WHEN OLD MR. BADGER LEARNED TO STAY AT HOME

THE first time Peter Rabbit saw Digger the Badger, he laughed at him. Yes, Sir, Peter laughed at him. He laughed until he had to hold his sides. When he got back to the dear Old Briar-patch, he told little Mrs. Peter all about Digger. That is, he told her all that he had seen, which was really very little indeed about Digger, as he found out later.

"I found him away over on the Green Meadows in a place where I have never been before, and I almost stepped on him before I saw him. You should have seen me jump. I guess it is lucky I did, too, for he certainly has got the wickedest-looking teeth, and I didn't like the way he snarled. Then at a safe distance I sat down and laughed. I just had to. Why, his legs are so short and his coat hangs down so on each side that he doesn't seem to have any legs at all. And as for shape, he hasn't any. He is so broad and flat that he looks as if something big and heavy had passed over him and rolled him out flat. But how he can dig! If Johnny Chuck should ever see him digging, Johnny would die of envy. I'm going over there again to learn more about him."

"You'd better stay at home and mind your own affairs," replied little Mrs. Peter tartly. "No good comes of poking into the affairs of other people."

This is true, and Peter knows it, but he just couldn't keep away from that part of the Green Meadows where he had discovered Digger the Badger. The more he saw of Digger, the greater became his curiosity about him. The less Peter can find out for himself about any one, the more curious he becomes, and all he could find out about Digger was that he slept most of the day, never went far from home, could dig faster than any one Peter had ever heard of, was short-tempered, and was treated with respect by all his neighbors, even Old Man Coyote, who seemed to know him very well.

All this made Peter more curious than ever, so one day, when Old Man Coyote happened along by the Old Briar-patch, Peter ventured to ask him about Digger the Badger. Old Man Coyote happened to be feeling in fine humor, for he had just eaten a good dinner. So he sat down just outside the dear Old Briar-patch, and this is what he told Peter:

"Digger is an old friend of mine, and I would advise you to treat him with the greatest respect, Peter, because if you don't, and he ever gets his claws on you, that will be the end of you. I wouldn't care to get in a fight with him myself, big as I am. You may have noticed that no one ever bothers him."

Peter nodded, and Old Man Coyote continued: "I don't know of any one who minds his own business and keeps his nose out of the affairs of other people as Digger does. Greatest homebody I know of, unless it's Johnny Chuck, and even Johnny wanders off once in a while. But Digger never gets very far from his own doorstep. Says there is no place like home, and he can't see what anybody wants to leave the best place in the world for, even if they can come back to it."

Mrs. Peter reached over and poked

Peter in the back, but he didn't even look at her. You know, she is always trying to keep Peter from roaming about so. Old Man Coyote went on with his story.

"It isn't because Digger is afraid. Goodness, no! I don't know of any one better able to take care of himself than Digger the Badger. I guess it is because his family always have been home-lovers. I've heard my grandfather tell how Digger's grandfather was just the same as Digger is, and how he had heard his grandfather say the same thing about Digger's grandfather's grandfather. They say that the very first Badger, who founded the family way back in the days when the world was young, started this home-staying habit, and that all Badgers ever since then have been just like him. Digger is terribly proud of his family and of old Mr. Badger, who founded it so long ago. I don't know as I wonder at it. Old Mr. Badger certainly had more sense than some of his neighbors.

"You see, when Old Mother Nature first turned him loose in the Great World, he felt that she had not been at all fair in her treatment of him. His legs were so short and he was so broad and flat that everybody or nearly everybody laughed at him and good-naturedly poked fun at him. He pretended not to care, but he did care, just the same. No one really likes to be laughed at for something he cannot help. Mr. Badger would watch his neighbors, Mr. Wolf and Mr. Fox and Mr. Rabbit and others, run and jump, and then he would try to do as they did, and he couldn't because his legs were so short and so clumsy. He would sit for hours admiring the graceful forms of his neighbors and comparing them with his own homely shape. He would wonder what Old Mother Nature could have been thinking of when she made him.

"But he didn't say so to her. No, indeed! He kept his thoughts to himself and never let his neighbors know that he envied them in the least. One day he wandered out from the Green Forest on to the Green Meadows. He liked it out there. He liked to look up and see so much of the blue, blue sky all at once. He liked to look off and see a long distance. Of course, he couldn't do that in the Green Forest because of the trees. He liked being by himself because he felt so sensitive about his homely shape. He discovered that if he lay down flat on his stomach when any one came near, he was always passed unnoticed. Being so broad and flat and altogether shapeless, he could remain unseen right out there on the open Green Meadows even when the grass was short, and that was something that Mr. Wolf and Mr. Fox and even little Mr. Rabbit couldn't do. It pleased him. He began to be less envious of his neighbors.

"Then one never-to-be-forgotten day the Red Terror, which men call fire, broke loose in the Green Forest, and all the little people fled before it. Across the meadows and past old Mr. Badger they raced, with fear in their eyes, and behind them came the Red Terror. A terrible fear sprang up in the heart of Mr. Badger. With those short legs he never in the world could run fast enough to escape. What should he do? What *could* he do? He looked at the great claws on his stout feet, and all in a flash an idea came to him. Perhaps if he dug a hole and crawled into it, the Red Terror would not find him. At once he began to dig, and how the dirt did fly! In just no time at all he was quite out of sight, and by the time the Red Terror had reached there, he was so far down in the ground that he didn't even feel the heat.

"When it was all over and the earth had cooled off so that he could come out, he sat on the pile of dirt in front of his hole and did some hard thinking. He looked at his stout legs and long claws, and all at once it came over him that Old Mother Nature had not been so unfair after all. She had provided him with a means to take care of himself which he wouldn't exchange with any of his neighbors for all their speed and better looks. Later, when he saw how some of them were worn out with running, and some of them even had burned places on their coats, the last bit of envy disappeared.

"'I guess,' said he to himself, 'Old Mother Nature has given each one special blessings, but she expects us to find them out for ourselves. I've found mine out, some of them, anyway, and I'll just get busy and look for the rest. I'm going straight over to the prettiest part of the Green Meadows where the Red Terror hasn't been and dig myself a house in the ground. There is no place like a good home, so what is the good of roaming around? My legs were not intended for that, and those who have got longer legs can do it if they want to.'

"He did just what he said he would do. He practised digging until he was the best digger of all the little people. The more he dug, the stouter and stronger his legs became, and soon he found that all his neighbors respected his strength, and none would quarrel with him. Because he could get plenty to eat near his home, he never went far from his doorstep, and from that time on he lived in perfect safety and contentment. He brought his children up to do the same thing, and if you should go over and ask Digger to-day, he would tell you that there is no place like home, and that he envies no one. I'm glad, however, that not every one agrees with him, or I should have hard work to get a living," concluded Old Man Coyote with a sly wink at Mrs. Peter.

IX

WHEN BOB WHITE WON HIS NAME

IX

WHEN BOB WHITE WON HIS NAME

THIS isn't the story of the Bob White you know, and yet when I think it over, I don't know but that it is, after all. It is the story of the first Bob White, the great-great-great-ever-so-great-grandfather of the Bob White you know and I know and everybody who ever has heard his whistle knows. It is a story of that long-ago time, way back in the beginning of things, when the world was young, and yet I guess it is just as much our own Bob White's story as it is his great-great-great-ever-so-great-grandfather's. You see, it is because of it, of what happened in that long-ago time, that Bob White *is* Bob White. So that makes it his story too, doesn't it? Anyway, I'll tell you the story and leave it to you to decide.

Old Mother West Wind told me the story, and she got it from Peter Rabbit, and Peter got it from—well, I don't know for sure, but I suspect he got it from Bob White himself. You know Peter and Bob White are great friends. They are very near neighbors. They are such near neighbors and such good friends that if it popped into Peter's funny little head to be curious about Bob White's affairs, he wouldn't hesitate an instant to ask Bob about them. Anyway, some one told Peter the story, and I like to think that that some one was none other than that brown-coated little whistler, Bob White the Quail, himself. Here is the story as Old Mother West Wind told it to me:

"Long, long ago, way back in the beginning of things, when the world was young, when the Green Meadows were new, and the Green Forest was new, and the Smiling Pool and the Laughing Brook and the Big River were new, and the little and big people whom Old Mother Nature put in them to live were new too, being the very first each of his kind, things were different, quite different from what they are now. Old Mother Nature was busier than she is now, and goodness knows she is busy enough these days. In fact, she is a million times busier than the busiest other person in all the Great World. If she wasn't, if she grew tired or lazy or careless or anything like that, I am afraid things would go so wrong with the Great World that they never, never could be righted again.

"But in these far-away days in the

beginning of things she was busier still. It is always easier to keep things going after they are once started than it is to start them, and Old Mother Nature was just starting things. So she started a great many of the little people off in life, and told them to make the best of things as they found them in the Great World and do as well as they could while she was attending to other matters.

"Now one of these little people was a plump little person in a coat of reddish-brown feathers. He was Mr. Quail, the great-great-great-ever-so-great-grandfather of all the Quails. To Mr. Quail, as to all the others, Old Mother Nature said: 'The Great World is new. There is a place in it for you, but you must find that place for yourself. There is work for you to do, but you must find out for yourself what it is. When you have real need of anything come to me, but don't bother me until you do have. No one who proves to be helpless or useless will live long. Now run along and prove whether or not you have a right to live.'

"So little Mr. Quail went out among the other people in the Great World to try and find his place. All the other people were trying to find their places, and some of them were having a dreadful time doing it. A great many began by trying to do just what their neighbors did, which was the very worst kind of a mistake. It was a pure waste of time. Worse still, it wasn't making a place in the work of the Great World. Little Mr. Quail's eyes were very bright, and he used them for all they were worth. His wits were quite as bright, and he used these the same way.

"'There are two things for me to

find out,' said he to himself, 'what I can't do and what I can do. The sooner I find out what I can't do, the more time I'll have to find out what I can do. I've got wings, and that must mean that Old Mother Nature intends me to fly. I'm glad of that. It must be fine to sail around up in the air and see all that is going on down below.'

"Up overhead Ol' Mistah Buzzard was sailing 'round and 'round, high up in the sky, with hardly a motion of his broad wings. Little Mr. Quail watched him a long time, and a great longing to do the same thing filled him. At last he sprang into the air, and right then he made a discovery. Yes, Sir, he made a discovery. He must beat his wings with all his might in order to stay in the air. When he stopped beating them and held them spread out as Ol' Mistah Buzzard did, he found that he simply sailed a little way straight ahead and then began to come down. He must keep those wings moving very fast or else come down to the ground. Then he made another discovery. In a very little while his wings were so tired that he just had to stop flying.

"Little Mr. Quail squatted in the grass and panted for breath. He was disappointed, terribly disappointed. 'It's plain to me that Old Mother Nature doesn't intend that I shall spend my time sailing about in the air,' said he. He scratched his pretty little head thoughtfully. 'I can fly pretty fast for a short distance,' he continued, talking to himself, 'but that is all. That must mean that I have been given wings for use only in time of need. There are some birds flitting about in a tree. They seem to be having a good time. I think I'll join them. If I can't sail about in the air, the next best thing will be flitting about in the trees.'

"So after he had rested a bit, little Mr. Quail flew to the tree where the other birds were flitting about, and there he made another disappointing discovery. Try as he would, he couldn't flit about as they did. Moreover, he didn't feel comfortable perched in a tree for any length of time. It made his toes ache to bend them around the branch on which he was sitting. He watched the other birds, and his bright eyes soon discovered that their feet were different from his feet. Their toes were made to clutch twigs and hold them there comfortably, while his were not. 'Old Mother Nature doesn't intend that I shall spend my time flitting about in trees,' said he sorrowfully, and flew down to the ground once more.

"Right away his feet felt better. All

the ache left them. It was good to be on the ground. Pretty soon he began to run about. It was good to run about. He felt as if he could run all day without getting tired. While hunting for food he discovered that if his toes were not made for perching in trees, they certainly were made for scratching over leaves and loose earth where stray seeds were hiding. Then he made still another discovery. His coat was just the right color to make it hard work for others to see him when he squatted down close to the ground. If an enemy did discover him, his stout little wings took him out of danger like a bullet.

"Little by little it came over him that he had found his place in the Great World, which was on the ground most of the time. But he remembered what Old Mother Nature had said about work to do, and this worried him a little.

One day he watched Mr. Toad catching bugs. Old Mr. Toad was grumbling. 'I can't keep up with these pesky bugs,' said he. 'When I get my stomach full, I have to wait for it to get empty again before I can catch any more. But *they* don't wait. *They* keep right on eating all the time, and there won't be any green things left if I don't have help.'

"Little Mr. Quail grew thoughtful. Then he started in to help Old Mr. Toad catch bugs so as to give the green things a chance to grow. He had found work to do, and he did it with all his might. He forgot he ever had wanted to sail around in the air or flit about in the trees. He had found his place in the Great World, and he had found work to do, and also he had found the secret of the truest happiness. He was so happy that he had to tell his neighbors about

"I can't keep up with these pesky bugs," said he.

it. So every morning, just before starting work, he would fly up on a stump and whistle with all his might; what he tried to say was, 'All-all's right! All-all's right!' But what his neighbors thought he said was, 'Bob-Bob White! Bob-Bob White!'

"So they promptly called him Bob White and loved him for the cheer which his clear whistle brought to them. When Old Mother Nature came to see how things were getting on, she found little Mr. Quail the happiest and the most useful of all the birds, and as she listened to his whistle, she smiled and said: 'I love you, Bob White, and all the world shall love you.' And all the world has loved him to this very day."

X

WHEN TEENY-WEENY BECAME GRATEFUL

X

WHEN TEENY-WEENY BECAME GRATEFUL

DID something move among the dead leaves along that old log, or was it the wind that stirred them? Peter Rabbit stared very hard trying to find out. Not that it made the least bit of difference to Peter. It didn't. If something alive had moved those leaves, that something was too small for Peter to fear it. Probably it was a worm or a bug. It might have been a beetle. That looked like a good place for beetles. There was Jimmy Skunk ambling down the Lone Little Path this very minute, and Jimmy always appeared to be looking for beetles. Peter stared harder than ever. A leaf moved. Another turned fairly over. There wasn't any wind just then. Dead leaves don't turn over of themselves, so there must be something alive there.

"What has Peter on his mind this morning to make him stare so?" asked Jimmy Skunk as he ambled up.

Peter grinned. "I was just wondering," said he, "if there are any fat beetles under that log over there. Those dead leaves along the side of it have a way of moving once in a while without cause that I can see. There! What did I tell you?"

Sure enough, a couple of leaves had moved. Jimmy Skunk's eyes brightened. He actually almost hurried over to that old log, and began to rake away the leaves. Suddenly he stopped and sniffed. At the same time Peter thought he saw something dart in at the hollow end of that log. It might have been a shadow, but Peter had a feeling that it wasn't. Jimmy Skunk sniffed once more and then deliberately turned his back on that old log, and with his nose turned up, his face the very picture of disgust and disappointment, he rejoined Peter.

> "Teeny Weeny, clever and spry,
> Disappears while you wink an eye,"

said Jimmy.

"Oh!" exclaimed Peter. "Is that who it was? I suppose he was hunting beetles himself. He's such a little mite of a fellow that I should think a good-sized beetle could almost carry him away. I declare to goodness, I don't see how any one so small manages to live! Danny Meadow Mouse and Whitefoot the Wood Mouse are small enough, but they are giants compared with Teeny Weeny the Shrew. They have a hard enough time keeping alive, and I should think that any one smaller would stand no chance at all."

"Do you know Teeny Weeny very well?" asked Jimmy.

"No," confessed Peter. "I've seen him only a few times and then had no more than a glimpse of him."

"And yet he lives right around here where you come and go every day," said Jimmy.

"I know it," replied Peter. "I suppose it is because he is so small. He can hide under next to nothing."

Jimmy grinned. "I don't see but what you've answered yourself," he chuckled. "It's because he is so small that Teeny Weeny manages to keep out of harm. He isn't very good eating, anyway, so I have heard say."

"Why? Because there isn't enough of him to make a bite?" asked Peter.

"No," replied Jimmy. "Of course I don't know anything about it, but I've heard those who do say that a Shrew doesn't taste good, and that no one who is at all particular about his food will touch one. I am told that Hooty the Owl hunts Teeny Weeny, but Hooty isn't at all particular, you know. If Teeny Weeny tastes the way he smells, I for one don't want to try him."

Peter laughed right out. He couldn't help it. The idea of Jimmy Skunk being fussy about smells was too funny.

"What are you laughing at?" demanded Jimmy, suspiciously.

"At the idea that any one so small can smell bad enough to make any difference," replied Peter. "I wonder how he comes to have that bad smell."

"It's a reward," replied Jimmy. "It's a reward handed down to him from the days when the world was young, and his great-great-great-ever-so-great-grandfather, the first Shrew, you know, who was also called Teeny Weeny, was given it by Old Mother Nature, because he had sense enough to be grateful and to tell her that he was."

"It's a story!" cried Peter. "It's a story, and you've just got to tell it to me, Jimmy Skunk."

"Say please," grinned Jimmy.

"Please, please, please, please," replied Peter. "If that isn't enough, I'll say it as many times more."

"I guess that will do, because after all it isn't so very much of a story," returned Jimmy, scratching his head as if he were trying to stir up his memory.

"It happened way back in the beginning of things that when Old Mother Nature had about finished making the birds and the animals, she had just a teeny weeny pinch of the stuff they were made of left over. Because she couldn't then and can't now bear to be wasteful, she started to make something. First she started to make it into a very tiny mouse. Then she changed her mind and started to make it into a tiny mole. Finally she changed her mind again and made it into something like each but not just like either, blew the breath of life into it, and set it free in the great world. That was Teeny Weeny, the first Shrew, and the smallest of all animals.

"For a while Teeny Weeny wished that he hadn't been made at all. He wished that Old Mother Nature hadn't been so thrifty and saving. What was the good of being an animal at all if he wasn't big enough to be recognized as such? That's the way he felt about it for a while. It hurt his feelings to have old King Bear say, after just missing him with his great foot, 'I beg your pardon. You are so tiny I thought you were a bug of some kind. Of course, I don't mind stepping on bugs, but I wouldn't step on you for the world. Why don't you grow so that we can see you?'

"'Yes, why don't you?' asked old Mr. Wolf. 'If you get stepped on, don't blame us.' Even Mr. Meadow Mouse laughed at him because he was so small. Teeny Weeny was quite furious at that. So for a while he was very unhappy because he was so small. He ate and ate and ate, hoping that this would make him grow bigger. But it didn't. He remained as small as ever, the smallest of all the four-footed people. And his temper didn't improve. Not a bit. He was fretful and snappish. He said all sorts of things about Old

Mother Nature because she had made him so small. He almost hated her. He couldn't see a single advantage in being so small.

"Time went on, and at length came the hard times of which you have heard, the times when food was so scarce and most of the little people were always hungry. Then it was that the big and strong began to hunt the small and weak, as you know. At first Teeny Weeny was in a regular panic of fear. He felt that because he was so small he hadn't any chance at all. But after a while he made a discovery, a most amazing discovery. It quite took his breath away when he first realized it. It was that because he was so small he had more chance than some of those of whom he had been envious. Because he was so small, he could slip out of sight in a twinkling. He could slip into holes that no one else could get into. A leaf on the ground would hide him.

"Then he discovered that because he was so very small, it didn't take much food to fill his stomach, and he had no trouble in finding all he needed to eat. While his neighbors were going hungry, he was fat and comfortable. Bugs there were and worms there were in plenty, and on these he lived. One day he saw Old Mother Nature, and she looked worried. She *was* worried. It was in the very middle of the hard times and wherever she went, the little people of the Green Forest and the Green Meadows crowded about her to complain and ask her help. Teeny Weeny remembered all the bitter things he had said and all the bitter thoughts he had had because she had made him so small, and he was ashamed. Yes, Sir, he was ashamed. You see, he realized by this time that his small size was his greatest blessing.

"What did Teeny Weeny do but march right straight up to Old Mother Nature the first chance he got and tell her how grateful he was for what she had done for him. He was quite honest. He told her how he had felt, and how he had said bitter things, and how sorry he was now that he understood how well off he was. Then he thanked her once more and turned to leave. Old Mother Nature called him back. She was wonderfully pleased to have these few words of thanks amid so many complaints.

"'Teeny Weeny,' said she, 'because you have been smart enough to see, and honest enough to admit a blessing in what you had thought a hardship, and because you have been grateful instead of complaining, I herewith give you this musky odor, which will be distasteful to even the hungriest of your enemies. It is a further protection to you and your children and your children's children for ever and ever.'

"And so it was, and so it has been, and so it is, and that's all," concluded Jimmy Skunk.

XI

WHEN OLD MR. HARE BECAME A TURNCOAT

XI

WHEN OLD MR. HARE BECAME A TURNCOAT

TURNCOAT isn't considered a very nice name to call any one. You see, it is supposed to mean one who has turned traitor, as it were; has been on one side and gone over to the other side. If a soldier who is fighting for France should go over to the German army and fight for Germany against France, he would be a turncoat. Benedict Arnold, of whom you have read in history, was a turncoat. But the meaning isn't always bad. Just take the case of Jumper the Hare. In summer he wears a coat of brown, but in winter he wears a coat of white, the white of the pure driven snow. So you see he is a turncoat, but in his case it doesn't mean anything bad at all. On the contrary, it means something rather nice and very interesting.

Now you know Jumper is the cousin of Peter Rabbit and looks very much like Peter, save that he is very much larger and has longer hind legs and longer ears. But Peter wears the same little homely brown coat in winter that he does in summer, the only difference being that it is thicker and so warmer. I am afraid that Peter has sometimes let a little envy creep into his heart when he has met his cousin wearing a coat of pure white. Be that as it may, Peter puzzled over the matter a great deal until he found out from Grandfather Frog how it happens that Jumper has such a lovely winter coat.

It happened one evening in early June, when Peter was hopping along down the Lone Little Path through the

Green Forest, that he met Jumper and stopped to gossip for a few minutes. He had not seen Jumper since gentle Sister South Wind had swept away the last of the winter snow. Then Jumper's coat had been white; now it was brown. This reminded Peter that he never had been able to tease Jumper into telling him how he could change his coat that way. None of Peter's other friends of the winter seemed to know, for he had asked all of them, and each had told him to ask Grandfather Frog. Of course, Peter couldn't do that in winter because Grandfather Frog was then fast asleep in the mud at the bottom of the Smiling Pool. With the coming of spring he had forgotten all about the matter. Now at the sight of Jumper once more, it all came back to him.

When Peter and Jumper parted,

Peter started for the Smiling Pool, lipperty-lipperty-lip. He arrived there quite out of breath. Grandfather Frog smiled a big, broad smile. Before Peter could say a word Grandfather Frog spoke.

"If you will catch a foolish green fly for me, Peter, I'll tell you the story," said he.

For a full minute Peter couldn't find his tongue, he was so surprised. "How do you know what story I want?" he stammered at last.

"I don't know, but that doesn't make any difference," replied Grandfather Frog. "Catch me a foolish green fly, and I'll tell you any story you want."

"But—but—but I can't catch foolish green flies," cried Peter. "I would if I could, but I can't, and you know I can't."

"You can try," replied Grandfather Frog gruffly, but with a twinkle in his eyes which Peter didn't see.

Peter hesitated. Then suddenly he shut his lips in a way that meant that he had made up his mind to something. He looked this way and that way. Whichever way he looked he saw foolish green flies flitting about. He jumped for one and missed it. He jumped for another and missed it. It was the beginning of such a funny performance that Grandfather Frog nearly rolled off his big green lily-pad with laughter. Peter raced and jumped this way and that way on the banks of the Smiling Pool as if he had gone quite crazy, and at last in his excitement jumped right into the Smiling Pool itself after a foolish green fly. But not one did he catch.

As he crawled out of the water, looking forlorn enough, Grandfather Frog took pity on him. "Chug-a-rum!" said he. "Lie down there in the sun and dry off, Peter, and I'll tell you the story."

"But I haven't caught you a foolish green fly!" exclaimed Peter.

"No, but you've tried, and willingness to try is just as deserving of reward as successful effort. Now what was it you wanted to know?" replied Grandfather Frog.

"If you please, I want to know how it is that my cousin, Jumper the Hare, happens to have a white coat in winter. It seems to me very curious," replied Peter.

"A long time ago, in the beginning of things," began Grandfather Frog, "Old Mother Nature gave the first Hare a brown coat and turned him out into the Great World to shift for himself, just as she had done with all the other animals. That was a very easy matter for old Mr. Hare, who wasn't old then, of course. You see, those were good times with plenty for all to eat without trying to eat each other. Mr. Hare was very bashful, and like most bashful people he liked to be by himself. So he made his home in the most lonely part of the Green Forest and was very happy and contented for a long time.

"Now being alone so much made him very timid, ready to jump and run at the least unusual sound, and this, it happens, proved to be a very good thing for Mr. Hare. You see, being by himself that way, he had plenty to eat even after the hard times of which you have heard had begun. So he was in splendid condition, was Mr. Hare, even after some of the other little people had begun to grow thin because of lack of food. One day Mr. Lynx happened to stray to that part of the Green Forest where Mr. Hare was living. He saw Mr. Hare before Mr. Hare saw him. He licked his lips hungrily. 'Ha!' thought he, 'this is where I get a good dinner.'

"With this he began to creep ever so softly towards Mr. Hare. But careful as he was, he stepped on a tiny stick and it snapped. Instantly away went Mr. Hare without stopping to see what had made the noise. That was because he had grown so timid from living so much alone. Then Mr. Lynx made a mistake. With a yell he started after Mr. Hare, and so Mr. Hare learned that it was no longer safe to trust his neighbors. Mr. Lynx didn't catch Mr. Hare, because Mr. Hare was too swift of foot for him, but he gave him such a scare that Mr. Hare was more timid than ever. Others tried to catch him, and, little by little, Mr. Hare learned that he must always be on the watch, and that safety lay in two things—his long legs and his brown coat. He learned about the latter by being surprised once by Mr. Wolf. He knew that Mr. Wolf didn't see him as he crouched among the brown leaves. For once he was too frightened to run, Mr. Wolf was so close to him, and this, as it happened, was a very good thing. Mr. Wolf trotted right past without seeing him or smelling him.

"After that Mr. Hare tried that trick often, for he was smart, was Mr. Hare. When he suspected that he had been seen he ran, but when he felt sure that he hadn't been seen, he sat tight right where he happened to be. But when the first snow came, Mr. Hare found himself in a peck of trouble. He didn't dare sit still when an enemy was near, because his brown coat stood out so against the white snow, and when he ran it was an easy matter to keep him in sight. One day he was squatting under a snow-covered hemlock bough when he was startled by the howl of Mr. Wolf not far away. In his fright he jumped up, and the next thing he knew down came the snow from the bough all over him. Then, to his dismay, he saw Mr. Lynx not two jumps away. He sat still from force of habit. Mr. Lynx didn't see him; he went right past Presently Mr. Wolf came along, and he went right past.

"Mr. Hare was puzzled. Then he just happened to glance at his coat. He was white with snow from head to foot! Then he understood, and a great idea popped into his head. If only he could have a brown coat in summer and a white coat in winter, he felt sure that he could take care of himself. He thought about it a great deal. Finally he screwed up his courage and went to Old Mother Nature. He told her all about how he had learned to sit tight when he wasn't seen, but that it didn't always succeed when there was snow on the ground. Then he told her how Mr. Lynx and Mr. Wolf had run right past him the time he was covered with snow. Very timidly he asked Old Mother Nature if she thought it possible that he might have a white coat in winter. Old Mother Nature said that she would think about it. It was almost the end of winter then, and he heard nothing from Old Mother Nature. With the coming of summer he quite forgot his request. But Old Mother Nature didn't. She kept an eye on Mr. Hare and she saw how timid he was and how he was in constant danger from his hungry neighbors. With the beginning of the next winter, Mr. Hare discovered one day that his coat was turning white. He watched it day by day and saw it grow whiter and whiter until it was as white as the snow itself. Then he knew that Old Mother Nature had not forgotten his request and at once hastened to thank her. And from that day to this, the Hares have had brown coats in summer and white coats in winter," concluded Grandfather Frog.

"Oh, thank you, Grandfather Frog," cried Peter with a little sigh of contentment. "I—I wish I could catch a foolish green fly for you."

"I'll take the will for the deed, Peter," replied Grandfather Frog. And he suddenly snapped up a foolish green fly that flew too near.

XII

WHEN GREAT-GRANDFATHER SWIFT FIRST USED A CHIMNEY

XII

WHEN GREAT-GRANDFATHER SWIFT FIRST USED A CHIMNEY

OF all his feathered friends and neighbors there was none whom Peter Rabbit enjoyed watching more than he did Sooty the Chimney Swift. There were two very good reasons why Peter enjoyed watching Sooty. In the first place Sooty always appeared to be having the very best of good times, and you know it is always a pleasure to watch any one having a good time. Ol' Mistah Buzzard, sailing and sailing high in the sky with only an occasional movement of his great wings, always seemed to be enjoying himself, and so did Skimmer the Swallow, skimming just above the tall grass of the Green Meadows or wheeling gracefully high in the air. But neither these two nor any other bird ever seemed to Peter to be getting so much real fun out of flying as Sooty the Swift. Just to hear him shout as he raced with swiftly beating wings and then glided in a short half circle was enough to make you want to fly yourself, thought Peter.

The second reason why Peter enjoyed watching Sooty was that he was very much a bird of mystery, in spite of the fact that Peter saw him every day through the long summer. You know, we all enjoy anything that is mysterious. To Peter there was no end of mystery about Sooty the Swift. He was not like other birds. In the first place he hardly looked like a bird at all. His tail was so short that it was hardly worth calling a tail. His neck was so short that his head seemed a part of his body. And then in all the time he had known him, Peter never had seen Sooty still for a single instant. Ol' Mistah Buzzard would come down from high up in the blue, blue sky and sit for hours on a dead tree in the Green Forest or walk about on the ground. Skimmer the Swallow would sit on the branch of a tree, or on the very top of Farmer Brown's barn, and twitter sociably. But Sooty the Swift was always in the air. At least, he always was whenever Peter saw him.

Sometimes Peter used to wonder if Sooty slept in the air as Ducks sleep on the water. Of course, he didn't really think that he did, but never seeing him anywhere but in the air, he was ready to believe almost anything. Then one evening just at dusk, Peter happened to be over in the Old Orchard close by Farmer Brown's house, and he saw something that puzzled him more than ever. He saw Sooty the Swift right above the chimney on Farmer Brown's house. It seemed to Peter as if something happened to Sooty. He beat his wings in a queer way, but instead of flying on, he dropped right straight down, down, down, and disappeared. He had fallen down that chimney! Peter waited a long time, but Sooty didn't appear again, and finally Peter went home with the feeling that he never again would see Sooty.

But he did see him again. He saw him the very next day, flying and shouting and seemingly having just as good a time as ever. It was then that Peter's curiosity would no longer be denied. He headed straight for the Smiling Pool to consult Grandfather Frog.

"He'll know all about Sooty if anybody does," thought Peter and hurried as fast as he could, lipperty-lipperty-lip. Grandfather Frog was in his usual place on his big green lily-pad. One glance told Peter that Grandfather Frog was in the best of humor, so he wasted no time.

"Grandfather Frog," cried Peter before he was fairly on the bank of the Smiling Pool, "I saw something queer last night, and you are the only one I know of who can tell me what it meant, because you are the only one I know who knows all about everything."

Grandfather Frog smiled. It was a great, big, broad smile. It pleased him to have Peter say that he knew everything. "Chug-a-rum! Not everything, Peter! I don't know everything. Nobody does," said he. "But if I happen to know what you want to know,

I'll be glad to tell you. Now what is it that is on your mind?"

Peter at once plunged into his story. He told Grandfather Frog how much he enjoyed watching Sooty fly and how little he knew about Sooty. He wound up by telling how he had seen Sooty fall down that chimney and how surprised he had been to see Sooty about the next day as well and happy as ever. He called Sooty a Swallow, for that is what Peter thought that Sooty was. He always had thought so.

When Peter had finished, Grandfather Frog chuckled. It was a long, deep chuckle that seemed to come clear from his toes. When he had enjoyed his chuckle to his heart's content, he looked up at Peter and blinked his great goggly eyes.

"What would *you* say, Peter, if I should tell you that Sooty isn't a member of the Swallow family at all?" he asked.

"I'd believe you," replied Peter promptly, "but I never again would dare guess what family anybody belonged to from his looks."

"Well, Sooty isn't a Swallow at all," said Grandfather Frog slowly. "He is a Swift, which is another family altogether. Furthermore, he didn't fall down that chimney. No, Sir, he didn't fall down that chimney. He flew down, and he did it because he lives there. Now listen, and I'll tell you a story."

Peter needed no second invitation. A story from Grandfather Frog is always one of Peter's greatest treats, as you know.

"Chug-a-rum!" began Grandfather Frog, as he always does. "When Old Mother Nature first peopled the Great World, she made each bird a little different from every other bird, and each animal a little different from every other animal. Then she turned them loose to make their way the best they could, and let them alone to test them and see how each would make the best of his advantages. Mr. Swift, the great-great-ever-so-great-grandfather of Sooty, felt at first as if Old Mother Nature had forgotten to give him any advantages at all. He was homely. There wasn't so much as a single bright feather in his whole coat. He had a tail which might as well have been no tail at all, so far as he could see. He had tiny feet on which he couldn't walk at all, and with which it was all he could do to hang on to a twig when he wanted to rest. But when it came to wings, he wasn't long in discovering that in these he was blessed beyond most of his neighbors. Those wings certainly were made for speed. They were long and narrow, and they drove him through the air faster than his neighbors with broader wings could fly and with a great deal less effort. He could fly all day without getting tired, and he never was so happy as when darting about high in the air.

"Of course, it didn't take him long to find out that he could catch all kinds of flying insects, and so he had no trouble in filling his stomach while flying, for his mouth was very wide. 'It must be,' thought he, 'that Old Mother Nature expects me to live in the air. I wish I could sleep while I am flying, but I can't. I never feel comfortable sitting on a twig.'

"One day he discovered that he could do something that no other bird could do. By using his wings in a certain way he could drop right straight down without really falling. He practised this a great deal just for fun. Then one day as he was flying over a rocky place, he saw right under him a great hole that went straight down into the ground. It interested him. He wondered what it was like inside. The more he wondered, the more he wanted to find out. So one day, after many trials, he dropped straight down into the hole by means of that new way of flying he had discovered.

"He didn't go very far down, because it was so dark in there, and he was beginning to get a wee bit frightened. On his way up he brushed against the side of the rocky wall and without knowing why, he put out both feet and clung to it, folding his wings for a minute's rest. Then he found that by pressing his funny little tail, which ended in sharp spines, against the wall, he rested more comfortably than ever he had before in all his short life. He could cling to a rough wall very much easier than he could sit on a perch. After that he spent his nights in that hole and was happy.

"A long time later he was far from home when night was coming on, and he knew that he wouldn't be able to get there before dark. Looking down as he flew, he saw the hollow trunk of a great tree which had been broken off by the wind. Why not sleep in that? He circled over it two or three times and then dropped straight down inside. He liked it. He liked it better than he did the hole in the rocks. After that he made his home in a hollow tree.

"In course of time old King Eagle led the birds to a new part of the Great World which Old Mother Nature had been preparing for them to spend the summer in. Mr. Swift went with the others. But when he got there, he could find no hole in the ground and no hollow tree. But he found something else. He found the queer homes of men and on top of each a straight, tall thing quite like a hollow tree, only all black inside and made of what seemed like stone. Having no other place to go, he tried one of them. The next day he searched for a hollow tree but could find none, and so returned to that chimney, for that is what it was. So it was every day. After a little he began to like the chimney. It was easy to get in and out of. No one ever bothered him there. It was easy to cling to the wall of it. At last he decided to build a nest there. And from that day to this, the Swifts have lived in the chimneys on the houses of men. When you thought you saw Sooty fall, he was simply going home to spend the night," concluded Grandfather Frog.

"Thank you," replied Peter with a long sigh. "It's a funny world, isn't it, Grandfather Frog? The idea of living in a chimney! The very idea!"

XIII

WHEN PETER RABBIT FIRST MET BLUFFER THE ADDER

XIII

WHEN PETER RABBIT FIRST MET BLUFFER THE ADDER

HOPPITY-SKIP down the Crooked Little Path, lipperty-lipperty-lip, went Peter Rabbit in his usual heedless, careless way. Peter never can seem to get it into his funny little head why he should be careful when there appears to be no particular reason for being careful. He is like a great many people—careful when he knows that there is danger near, but as heedless as you please when he thinks that all is safe. He has got to see or hear danger before he will believe that it is near. Like a lot of other folks he has yet to wake up to the fact that the only way to keep out of trouble is to be always prepared for trouble.

So Peter hopped and skipped down the Crooked Little Path, as he had a thousand times before, without a thought of danger. Nothing ever had happened to him on the Crooked Little Path, and so he thought nothing ever could. Suddenly as he rounded a little turn, there was a sound that made Peter stop so suddenly that he almost fell over backward—a sound that made every hair on his body stand on end and his eyes pop out with fright. It was a hiss, the loudest, most awful hiss he ever had heard. For just a second Peter was too frightened to move. There, coiled up right in the Crooked Little Path, was a member of the Snake family whom he never had seen before. And such a fierce, ugly-looking fellow as he was! No wonder Peter was frightened. This Snake had the flattest head Peter ever had seen. His body was rather short and thick, and his neck was flattened in a way that made it appear very large and gave to him a very ugly and dangerous look.

As soon as he could get his wits together, Peter turned and raced pell-mell up the Crooked Little Path as fast as his long legs would take him. Looking behind him he didn't see in front of him, and so he almost ran into Jimmy Skunk. In fact, he would have, if Jimmy hadn't cried:

"Hi, there! Why don't you look where you are going? What is the matter with you, anyway, Peter Rabbit?"

Peter was so startled by Jimmy that he jumped to one side as if he suddenly had stepped on something hot. Then he saw who it was. "Oh, Jimmy," he cried, "you mustn't go down the Crooked Little Path!"

"Why not?" demanded Jimmy Skunk, staring at Peter and noting how frightened Peter was.

"Because," panted Peter, "right down there in the middle of it is one of Mr. Black Snake's cousins, and I know by his looks that he is one of the dangerous kind, like Buzztail the Rattler. Ugh! I nearly ran into him, and he hissed enough to make your hair rise. He's got a terrible temper. I wouldn't go near him again for the world. Where are you going, Jimmy?"

"Down the Crooked Little Path to have a look at this terrible fellow," replied Jimmy over his shoulder. "Perhaps I can teach him some manners."

"Oh, Jimmy, do be careful!" begged Peter. "He really is very terrible. I know his bite must be awful. I guess it is worse than that of Buzztail the Rattler. I wouldn't go if I were you."

"I'm not such a fraidy as you, Peter," replied Jimmy Skunk, and ambled on down the Crooked Little Path. Peter wasn't sure about it, but he thought he heard Jimmy chuckle. That settled matters for Peter. If Jimmy was laughing at him for warning him of danger, he could just go on and get a good fright. It would serve him right. Peter hesitated a minute, then at a safe distance he followed. He wanted to see Jimmy Skunk when he rounded that little turn in the Crooked Little Path and heard that terrible hiss.

Jimmy ambled along slowly, for you know he never hurries. Presently he disappeared around that little turn, and right away Peter heard that terrible hiss. He expected to see Jimmy come racing back, and he was all ready to make fun of him for pretending to be so brave. But Jimmy didn't come. Once more Peter heard that angry hiss and felt his hair rise on end. Then all was still.

Peter waited as long as he could stand it, and then his curiosity got the best of him. Slowly and carefully he tiptoed along until he could see around the turn in the Crooked Little Path. What he saw quite took his breath away. There sat Jimmy Skunk looking down at something stretched out at his feet. It was that dreadful Snake on his back, and he appeared to be quite dead. Jimmy reached out and poked him, but Mr. Snake didn't move. Jimmy poked him some more, and still he didn't move.

"Oh, Jimmy, however did you dare to try to kill him?" cried Peter.

Jimmy reached out and poked him, but Mr. Snake didn't move.

Jimmy looked back at Peter and grinned. "Come on with me, and I will tell you a story," said he.

Peter hesitated, but the thought of a story was too much for him, and he followed Jimmy down the Crooked Little Path, taking pains to go around the body of Mr. Snake and not very near it at that, although he knew it was silly and foolish to be afraid of one who was dead. Jimmy didn't go far. He sat down and waited for Peter to join him. From where they were they could see the body of Mr. Snake stretched out on its back in the Crooked Little Path. Somehow, now that he was dead, Mr. Snake didn't look so very fierce and terrible. In fact he didn't look nearly so big as he had when he was alive. Peter was thinking of this when his heart gave a funny little jump. He had turned his head for just a second and now, as he looked back at Mr. Snake, he felt that his eyes must be playing him tricks for Mr. Snake was on his *stomach* instead of on his *back!*

Peter opened his mouth to say something, but Jimmy made a sign to keep still. So Peter kept still and with popping eyes watched Mr. Snake. Presently he saw Mr. Snake's head come up a little at a time and then move from side to side as if Mr. Snake were looking to see that the way was clear. Slowly Mr. Snake began to glide forward. Then, as if satisfied that no one was watching, he moved faster as if in a hurry to get away from there, and in a moment he disappeared.

Peter gulped two or three times as if trying to swallow the truth and then turned to stare at Jimmy Skunk. Jimmy laughed right out because Peter looked so funny.

"You—you didn't kill him, after all," gasped Peter.

"No," replied Jimmy, "I didn't even touch him until you saw me poke him when he lay there on his back."

Peter looked quite as puzzled as he felt. "Was he just pretending to be dead the way Unc' Billy Possum does?" demanded Peter.

Jimmy nodded. "You've guessed it," he replied.

"But why did he do it?" persisted Peter, such a puzzled look on his face that Jimmy just had to laugh again.

"Because he was afraid and tried to fool me into thinking him dead so that I would leave him alone," replied Jimmy.

"Afraid! That fellow afraid!" exclaimed Peter in an unbelieving tone of voice. "Why, when I saw him first, he was the most savage, dangerous-looking fellow that ever I have met."

Once more Jimmy laughed. "All in his looks, Peter," said he. "Yes, Sir, all his fierceness is in his looks. Really he is one of the most harmless and gentle fellows in the world. He tried to scare me just as he frightened you, and when he found it wouldn't work, he tried the other plan—pretended that he was dead. No one but Old Mr. Toad has the least reason in the world to be afraid of him. All his fierceness is just pretending, and that is how he comes by his name, which is Bluffer the Puff-Adder. I'm surprised that you've never happened to meet him before. I believe some folks call him the Hog-nosed Snake. I always like to meet him just to see him try to scare me, and when he finds he can't, I do a little pretending myself and give him a little scare by pretending that I am going to fight him. Then he always rolls over on his back and pretends that he is dead. I suppose he is chuckling to himself now because he thinks that he fooled us. The next time you meet him just show him that you know he is perfectly harmless and see how quickly he'll stop pretending that he is so ugly and dangerous. He learned that trick of bluffing from his father, and his father learned it from his father, and so on way back to the days when the world was young. I would tell you the story now if I had time, but I haven't."

"Then you'll have to do it some other time," retorted Peter, "for I shall give you no peace until you do."

XIV

WHEN MR. WOOD MOUSE LEARNED FROM THE BIRDS

XIV

WHEN MR. WOOD MOUSE LEARNED FROM THE BIRDS

PETER RABBIT never will forget the first time that he saw Whitefoot the Wood Mouse pop out of a nest in a bush a few feet above his head. It wasn't so much the surprise of seeing Whitefoot as it was the discovery that that nest was Whitefoot's own. Peter had seen that nest often. It was in a bush just a little above one of Peter's favorite paths on the edge of the Green Forest. Always he had supposed that it belonged to one of his feathered friends. He had seen many such nests. At least, he supposed he had. That was because he hadn't taken the trouble to look at this one particularly. He hadn't used his eyes. If he had, he might have seen that this, while very like other nests he had seen, was different. It was different in that it had a roof. Yes, Sir, this particular nest had a roof. And it had a doorway, a very small doorway, and this doorway was underneath, a very queer place for a bird to make a doorway had there been any bird of his acquaintance who would build a roof to a nest, anyway. All of which goes to show how easy it is to see things without really seeing them at all.

It was just at dusk that Peter happened along this particular little path and saw Whitefoot the Wood Mouse pop out of that nest.

"Hello!" exclaimed Peter. "What are you doing up there? What business have you in that nest? Have you been stealing eggs?"

"No, I haven't been stealing eggs," retorted Whitefoot indignantly. "And if I haven't any business in this nest I should like to know who has. It's my nest! Who has a better right in it?"

"Your nest!" exclaimed Peter. "Why, I thought you lived in a hollow tree or a hollow log or a hole in the ground or some such place. How long is it since you learned to build a nest like a bird, and who taught you?"

Whitefoot knew by the tone of Peter's voice that Peter didn't believe a word of what he had been told. He looked very hard at Peter, and in his big, soft, black eyes was an indignant look which Peter couldn't help but see. "I don't care whether you believe it or not, this is my nest, and I built it," said he indignantly. "At least I built it over," he added, for Whitefoot is very truthful. "In the winter I do live in a hollow tree or a hollow log or a hole in the ground, whichever is most comfortable, but in the warm weather I have a summer home, and this is it. My family has known how to build such homes ever since the days of my great-great-ever-so-great-grandfather when the world was young. It was he who learned the secret, and it has been in our family ever since."

Peter's long ears stood straight up with excited interest and curiosity. "Tell me about it!" he begged. "Tell me how your great-great-ever-so-great-grandfather learned how to build a nest like a bird. Please tell me, Whitefoot."

Whitefoot sat up and daintily washed his pretty white hands. "I don't think I will," he replied slowly. "You didn't believe me when I said that this nest is mine, and so I'm sure you won't believe the story of my great-grandfather. I don't like telling stories to people who don't believe."

"But I will believe it!" cried Peter. "If you say it is true, I'll believe every word of it. Please tell me the story, Whitefoot. Oh, please do." Peter was very much in earnest. "I'm sorry I didn't believe you at first when you said that this nest is yours. But I do now, Whitefoot. I do now. Please, please tell me the story."

Whitefoot's black eyes snapped and twinkled. He enjoyed being teased for that story. You see, he is such a little fellow, such a very little fellow, that his bigger neighbors seldom take any notice of him unless it is to try to catch him. There are several who would be glad to swallow Whitefoot if they could catch him. So, being such a little fellow, he felt rather puffed up, rather important, you know, that Peter Rabbit should be so interested and should actually be begging him for a story. He climbed up to a crotch in a tree just a little above Peter's head, a place where he could watch out for danger, made himself comfortable with his back against the trunk of the tree, carefully combed his fur, for Whitefoot is very particular how he looks, and then began his story.

"Always, ever since the world was young, Mice have been among the smallest of the little people of the Green Meadows and the Green Forest, and because of this they have had to live by their wits if they would live at all. In the beginning of things it was not so, I have heard it said, because then there was plenty for all to eat and no cause for the big and strong to seek to kill the small and weak. But when the hard times came and hunger led to the doing of many dreadful things, all of the Mouse tribe found that they were in danger all the time, just as they are to-day.

"My great-great-great-grandfather, the first of all the Wood Mice, chose the Green Forest for his home instead of the Green Meadows where his cousin, old Mr. Meadow Mouse, liked best to live. He chose the Green Forest because it was always beautiful there, and because among the roots of the trees and in the trees themselves there were so many hiding-places. He was very small, just as I am, and he was very smart."

"Just as you are?" inquired Peter with a twinkle in his eyes.

"I didn't say that!" retorted Whitefoot indignantly. "I never have claimed to be very smart, though I've been smart enough to keep out of the clutches of Reddy Fox and Hooty the Owl and all the others who hunt me. But great-great-great-grandfather *was* smart. In the Green Forest he had prepared for himself many hiding-places. Some were in the ground, some were in holes in trees, and some were in hollow stumps and logs. For a while he felt quite safe and easy in his mind, even when the times had become so hard and food so scarce that night and day some of his big neighbors like Mr. Lynx and Mr. Fox and Mr. Wolf and Mr. Owl and Mr. Hawk and even old King Bear were sure to come prowling about looking for little people like himself. You see, he had plenty to eat himself because he had been forehanded and had stored away seeds in some of his hiding-places. And he felt perfectly safe because the doorways to his hiding-places were so very small that none of these people could follow him into them.

"So he used to laugh at those who hunted him and sometimes would dodge into one of his little doorways right under their very noses. But one day he saw old King Bear tear open an old hollow stump with his great claws, and he knew that King Bear was looking for him. Another day quite by chance he happened to see Mr. Weasel slip into one of his smallest doorways, and then a great fear took hold of Grandfather Wood Mouse. His enemies knew now where to look for him and how to get into his hiding-places; they were no longer safe.

"'I must find a new hiding-place and keep it a secret,' thought he. For many days he went about, thinking and thinking. One day he had this very much on his mind as he watched Mr. Catbird build a nest. All in a flash a great idea came to him. If he could have a home in a bush like that of Mr. Catbird, no one ever, ever would think of looking for him there! 'If birds can build nests, why can't I?' thought he. All that day he watched the building of Mr. Catbird's nest, trying to see just how each stick was placed and how the nest was lined with fine roots and grass and strips of grapevine bark. The next day he hunted up some old nests in bushes not too high above the ground and climbed up to them. He even pulled some of them to pieces to see how they were made and then tried to put them together again.

"'I believe I can do it!' he exclaimed over and over to himself. 'I believe I can do it! Anyway, it will do no harm to try. No harm can come of trying.'

"He remembered an old nest in a bramble bush not far from where he lived. This he examined very carefully. It would do for a foundation. Then he went to work, taking care to build only when no one was near to discover his secret. He brought grass and fine roots, and he made that nest more comfortable than it had been when it was first built. Then he built a roof over it, so that it would shelter him in bad weather, and to get into it he made a little round doorway. When it was finished, he was very proud of it, as he had reason to be. He carried seeds into it, and then he made it his home for the summer and way into the fall. Of course, no one ever dreamed of looking for him in what seemed like a bird's nest, and many a time he peeped out and watched his hungry neighbors walk right under him without ever suspecting that he was near.

"Of course, he taught his children the secret of nest-building which he had learned from the birds, and that has been the most precious secret in our family ever since. You won't tell any one, will you, Peter?" he concluded anxiously.

"No," said Peter, "I won't tell any one. Of course I won't. It must be nice to have a sort of sky-parlor in the summer," he added wistfully.

"It is," replied Whitefoot. "I just love my summer home." With this he climbed up to his snug nest, and the last Peter saw of him was his long slim tail disappearing through the little round doorway.

XV

WHEN MR. HUMMINGBIRD GOT HIS LONG BILL

XV

WHEN MR. HUMMINGBIRD GOT HIS LONG BILL

"I saw him here; I saw him there;
And now he is not anywhere!
He is not there; he is not here,
Yet no one saw him disappear."

PETER RABBIT didn't intend that for any ears but his own, but it never is safe to talk out loud if you want no one else to hear.

"Huh!" said a voice right back of Peter. Peter started ever so little and hastily turned his head, but saw no one.

"Huh!" said the voice again. "Huh! Are you a poet, Peter Rabbit?"

This time Peter turned wholly around in a single jump. Staring up at him from under a mullein-leaf was Old Mr. Toad.

"What's a poet?" demanded Peter.

"A poet is some one who—who—Say, Peter Rabbit, have you eaten something that went to your head?" Old Mr. Toad looked really anxious.

"No," replied Peter, "it went to my stomach. Everything I eat goes to my stomach."

"Then it can't be that you are a real poet," sighed Old Mr. Toad. "I was a little afraid you might be when I overheard you just now. On the whole I am rather glad, Peter. It would be so tiresome to have to listen to you talking that way. By the way, who is it that is not there and is not here, yet no one saw him disappear?"

"Hummer the Hummingbird," replied Peter eagerly. "You see him in one place and before you can get your mouth open to speak, he is somewhere else. Then in a shake of your tail he isn't anywhere at all. I mean he isn't anywhere in sight."

"I haven't any tail," retorted Old Mr. Toad rather testily. "I got rid of the silly thing long ago, as you very well know, Peter Rabbit."

"Excuse me, Mr. Toad. I didn't mean anything personal. It was just a way of speaking to show how quickly Hummer disappears. I was thinking of my own tail," said Peter.

"Huh!" grunted Old Mr. Toad just as before. "Then you weren't thinking of much."

Peter laughed. "Not so very much," he replied. "Still I can shake it, even if there isn't much of it. See!" He stood up and twitched his funny little tail until solemn Old Mr. Toad had to laugh in spite of himself.

"Hummer is such a wonderful little fellow," continued Peter eagerly. "He is so tiny it doesn't seem possible that he can be like other birds. I don't feel really acquainted with him because he isn't still long enough for me to more than nod to him."

"That's true," replied Old Mr. Toad, nodding sagely. "He isn't still down near the ground, but if you happened to find his home, you would often see him sitting near it as still as any other bird. By the way, Peter, did you ever hear how it happened that he comes by such a long bill?"

"A story!" cried Peter, jumping up and down and clapping his hands. "Oh, Mr. Toad, I never did hear, and I'm just dying to know. Please do tell me!"

There was a twinkle in Old Mr.

Toad's beautiful eyes,—for they really are beautiful, you know. He backed a little farther under the big mullein-leaf where the sun couldn't reach him, opened and closed his big mouth two or three times without making a sound, rolled his eyes back as if he were looking way, way into the past, and then, just as Peter had begun to think that there wasn't going to be any story after all, he began to talk in a funny little voice that seemed to come from way down where his throat and his stomach meet.

"It was long, long, long ago," said he.

"I know! It was way back when the world was young," interrupted Peter eagerly.

"Oh! So you know the story after all, do you?" grunted Old Mr. Toad rather crossly.

"I beg your pardon. I do indeed. I'm sorry," Peter hastened to say.

"Very well. Very well," grumbled Old Mr. Toad, "but don't do it again. Now I'll have to begin all over again. It was a long, long, long time ago in the beginning of things when Old Mother Nature had made all the big birds and the middle-sized birds and the little birds that she discovered that she had just a teeny, weeny bit of the things birds are made of left over. There wasn't enough to make even the head of an ordinary bird. No bird had use for another head, anyway.

"Now Old Mother Nature never could bear to waste anything, and she didn't intend to begin. So she made a teeny, weeny bird and she made him just as perfect as any other bird. She gave him feathers just like any other bird, only of course his feathers were teeny, weeny. She gave him a tail just like any other bird, only it was a teeny, weeny tail. She gave him feet with toes and claws just like any other bird, only they were teeny, weeny feet. And she gave him a bill, only it was a teeny, weeny bill and it was short. And because he was so teeny, weeny and yet a perfect bird, Old Mother Nature was very proud of him, so she gave him a beautiful green coat. The beautiful ruby throat was not given him until later, when he proved so brave of heart and so loyal to King Eagle, you remember."

"I remember," said Peter. "He got his ruby throat when old King Eagle won his crown of white."

"When Old Mother Nature sent little Mr. Hummingbird out into the Great World to join the other birds, she told him that tiny as he was she could treat him no differently from the others, and that he would have to take care of himself and prove that he was worthy to live and have a place in the work of the Great World, for that was a law which she could not break for any one, great or small.

"So little Mr. Hummingbird darted away to join the other birds and find a place for himself in the Great World. When the other birds first saw him, they laughed at him because he was so tiny, and made fun of him, though truth to tell some of them were envious because of his beautiful coat, and others were envious because of the way in which he could dart about, for not one among them could fly so swiftly as little Mr. Hummingbird.

"Tiny though he was, he was stout of heart and fairly bursting with spunk. He would dash into the very faces of those who tried to tease him and would be away again before they could so much as strike at him. So it wasn't long before they let him alone, though among themselves they still looked on him as a joke and were sure he would not live long. Being such a teeny, weeny fellow, of course Mr. Hummingbird had a teeny, weeny stomach, and he soon discovered that he couldn't eat the things that other birds did but must hunt for teeny, weeny things. It didn't take him long to find out that there were many teeny, weeny insects just suited to him, especially about the flowers. So Mr. Hummingbird spent most of his time darting about among the flowers catching teeny, weeny insects to fill his teeny, weeny stomach.

"One day he paused in front of a deep-throated flower and discovered that many teeny, weeny insects had hidden in the heart of it. Try as he would he could not reach them. Now his own swift little wings were not quicker than Mr. Hummingbird's temper, and he promptly pulled that flower to pieces. Then he caught all the insects, and in doing this he discovered that in the heart of the flower were sweet juices, better than anything he ever had tasted before. After that he wasted no time hunting for teeny, weeny insects in the air, but darted from one deep-throated flower to another, pulling them to pieces and filling his teeny, weeny stomach with the insects hiding there and the sweet juices.

"One day along came Old Mother Nature to see how things were going. On every side were beautiful flowers torn to rags. She threw up her hands in dismay. 'Dear me!' she cried. 'I wonder who can have been doing such dreadful mischief!'

"Just then she caught sight of little Mr. Hummingbird tearing another flower to pieces. Sternly she called him before her, and he came fearlessly. 'Why are you tearing my beautiful flowers to pieces?' she demanded.

"'Because it is the only way I can get the food in the hearts of them, and it is the food best suited to me,' replied little Mr. Hummingbird promptly but respectfully.

"Old Mother Nature tried to look severe, but a twinkle crept into her eyes. Secretly she was pleased with the fearlessness of the teeny, weeny bird.

"'That may be, but I cannot have my beautiful flowers destroyed this way. It will never do at all!' said she.

She scratched her head thoughtfully for a few minutes. Then she reached out and took hold of Mr. Hummingbird's teeny, weeny bill. 'Pull,' said she. Little Mr. Hummingbird pulled with all his might, and his bill was pulled out until it was long and slender, and his tongue was pulled out long with it.

"'Now,' said Old Mother Nature, 'I guess you won't have to pull my flowers to pieces.'

"Little Mr. Hummingbird darted away to the nearest deep-throated flower and found that he could reach the teeny, weeny insects and the sweet juices without the least trouble, and from that time on he took the greatest care not to hurt the beautiful flowers. That is how Hummer, whom you know, happens to have a long bill," concluded Old Mr. Toad.

"And I suppose that is why he seems

to love the flowers so," said Peter as he looked down at Old Mr. Toad thoughtfully.

"It is," replied Old Mr. Toad, and yawned sleepily.

XVI

WHEN OLD MR. BAT GOT HIS WINGS

IT happens that the Merry Little Breezes, who, as you know, are the children of Old Mother West Wind, are quite as fond of stories as is Peter Rabbit. In fact, whenever they suspect that Peter is going to ask some one for a story, they manage to be about so that they may hear it too. Now the Merry Little Breezes are very fond of Grandfather Frog and many, many times they have helped him get a good dinner by blowing foolish green flies within his reach. It was after one of these times that Grandfather Frog promised them a story.

Now the Merry Little Breezes did not

intend to let Grandfather Frog forget that promise, so one afternoon when they had grown tired of romping on the Green Meadows, they danced over to the Smiling Pool and settled around the big, green lily-pad on which Grandfather Frog was dozing. All together they shouted:

"We know you're old;
We know you're wise;
And what you say
We dearly prize.
So tell a tale
Of olden days,
And then, mayhap,
We'll go our ways."

"Chug-a-rum! What shall it be about?" demanded Grandfather Frog, waking up quite good-natured.

"Tell us why Flitter the Bat can fly when none of the other animals can," cried one of the Merry Little Breezes.

Grandfather Frog cleared his throat

several times, and then he began, and this is the story he told:

"Once upon a time when the world was young, old Mr. Bat, the many times great-grandfather of Flitter, whom you all know, lived in a cave on the edge of the Green Forest. Old Mr. Bat was little, quite as little as Flitter is now. He didn't have any wings then. No, Sir, old Mr. Bat had no wings.

"Now old Mr. Bat's teeth were small and not made for cracking hard seeds and things of that sort, so he lived mostly on insects. He used to hunt for them under sticks and stones. Sometimes he had hard work to find enough for a meal, because, you know, so many other Green Forest people were hunting for them too.

"Now old Mr. Bat's eyes were very small, very, very small indeed, and the bright sun hurt them. So old Mr. Bat used to stay in his cave all day and hunt for his meals only after jolly Mr. Sun had gone to bed behind the Purple Hills. When he did come out, most of the crawling bugs had been caught by others, and it was hard work finding them. So often Mr. Bat went hungry.

"One evening old Mr. Bat noticed that at twilight a great many bugs fly about. He sat on a big stone at the mouth of his cave and watched. It seemed to him that the air was full of bugs. By and by a big fat fellow came so near that old Mr. Bat forgot where he was and jumped for him—jumped right off the top of the big stone. Of course he got a hard tumble, but he didn't mind it a bit, not a bit, for he had caught the bug. After that, old Mr. Bat used to spend most of the time he was awake jumping for flying bugs.

"One night he made a very long jump from a very high stone and got such a fall that all the breath was knocked out of his funny little body. When he had gotten his breath back he discovered that some one was looking down and smiling at him. It was Old Mother Nature.

"'Pretty hard work to get a dinner that way, isn't it, Mr. Bat?' asked Old Mother Nature.

"Mr. Bat allowed that it was.

"'How would you like to fly?' asked Old Mother Nature.

"Mr. Bat thought that that would be very fine indeed, but that was quite out of the question because, as you know, he hadn't any wings.

"Old Mother Nature said no more, but something seemed to be pleasing her greatly as she left Mr. Bat.

"The next evening when old Mr.

Bat awoke, he really didn't know whether he was himself or not. No, Sir, he didn't. His legs were much longer than they used to be and really of no use at all for walking. Between them was a queer thin skin. He couldn't run. He couldn't even crawl very well.

"At last, after much work, he managed to get to the top of a big rock. He was very hungry, and when a big, fat bug came along, he forgot all about his troubles and tried to jump. But instead of jumping as he always had, he just tumbled off the big rock. As he fell he spread out his legs. What do you think happened? Why, old Mr. Bat found that he could fly!

"And ever since that long-ago time the Bats have lived in dark caves and have been able to fly," concluded Grandfather Frog.

"Splendid!" cried the Merry Little Breezes. "And we thank you ever and ever so much!" Then they had a race to see who could be the first to blow a foolish green fly over to Grandfather Frog.

THE END